# SIMON

## STEELE RIDERS MC 2ND GENERATION
### BOOK 3

## C.M. STEELE

THE STEELE PRESS

Simon had pushed Vivian away more times than she could count, not because he didn't want her, but because he craved her too much. Timing mattered. They were young... and Vivian was far too young for the future he envisioned for them. So he waited, holding back his obsession until the moment was right.

But one more rejection, and the interference of another woman, was enough to break her heart for good. In a moment of pain and pride, Vivian lashed out with words she could never take back:

*"I hope we never see each other again. Forget you ever knew me, and I'll do the same."*

She never imagined those would be the last words she'd say to him before tragedy struck.

Now, Simon has woken from a coma with no memory of that fateful weekend — the weekend that shattered them both. He doesn't remember her anger, her tears, or the cruel goodbye. But Vivian remembers every second... and the guilt is eating her alive.

Can they rebuild what was lost when the past is a wound only she can feel? Or will the truth of that night destroy their second chance before it begins?

# CHAPTER ONE

## SIMON

I SPEED DOWN THE ROAD ON MY MOTORCYCLE, GOING FOR MY morning ride. I drive through town for a good hour while everyone is just beginning their day. I see some of my family and friends out and about, but there is one person I'm hoping is where she's supposed to be. I ride past Law's house, catching sight of Trouble's vehicle parked outside. That gives me a little peace of mind that she's home. We're on winter break from school, and soon I'll head back to finish my automotive engineering degree while she finishes her senior year of high school. She turns eighteen next month.

As much as I love staying home, I can't wait to get back—and Trouble is the only reason. She's the reason I lie awake at night, ride on my motorcycle more than I should, work out twenty hours a week, and call home way too fucking much.

1

I have way too many opportunities to run into Vivian Lawrence over the coming weeks, especially if we do a large Steele Riders holiday feast. I roll my eyes just thinking about that. I love my friends and family, but seeing Vivian is fucking torture. The day she turned sixteen was like a damn switch flipped on me, and then I'd been so obsessed that I snarled at every boy and man that breathed near her until I spoke to her father that summer.

It's been almost two years of obsession, and I can't do anything about it. What's worse is that I know she wants me as much as I want her. In fact, she's done her best to flirt with me as often as possible, teasing me to the point that I almost kissed her. Instead, I insulted her and told her to go home and grow up. Sometimes I regret those words, and sometimes they're the only thing keeping the distance between us.

I pulled into the auto body shop lot and parked my bike. As I do, my dad calls out and says, "What's up, Son? It's good to see you here so early."

"Yeah, early," I scoff, checking my watch. It's already ten, and they've all been here for three hours at least.

"Well, you're on vacation," he reminds me, like he has for the past several days. It's a force of habit, I suppose. Working hard is something that's been ingrained in me since I was a little kid, and he has no one to blame but himself.

"I need to earn my spending money," I tease. He gives me money to spend while I'm away, but I don't do shit besides focus on my obsession, and that doesn't cost a dime.

Besides, we all have trust funds, and I've been earning my keep for years working in the shop. He's been storing money away for me since I was ten.

"Come on. I've got an engine to rebuild. Show me what you've learned." I smirk and rub my hands together. This is going to be a great day.

We work hard for the next two hours, and I lose some of my outerwear until I'm down to my undershirt and jeans. It's the middle of December, but it doesn't matter because we're just south of Dallas, so it's in the mid-sixties.

My dad and I are having a blast.

"Need a drink?" he asks me.

"Yeah," I answered from under the engine block. We're taking our time because we can. I know it as much as he does. Yes, there are other projects on my father's list, but we don't spend that much time together anymore. I love my dad, and one day I'd love to share this with my son, if I have one.

He hands me a cold glass of sweet tea that I'm sure my mom prepared for us. "This is perfect."

"Tell me about it. That woman is a godsend," he says with a happy sigh. When I look at Vivian, that's what I see and feel. It's like the happiness my parents share. My chest burns with an ache I can't explain, and I want to be with her.

I set the glass down and pick up a wrench, getting back to work. We're almost done when something catches my attention out of the corner of my eye.

"Uh-oh," I grumble, picking up my grease towel and wiping my hands while staring at the front. At least once a week, she makes a damn excuse to come to the shop. She doesn't even have a problem with her car, so there is no reason for her to be here. If she did have an issue, her father or brother would bring it in. It's bullshit, and it's a distraction I don't need.

"What is it?" my father asks, following my gaze.

"Trouble." My attention is laser focused on the door. Standing there is the most beautiful and most frustrating girl ever—Vivian. She's been following me around everywhere, trying to draw me in so that I would make a critical error that would get us both in trouble; hence the reason I forever call her Trouble.

"What are you doing here, Vivian?" I bite out. She can't fathom how much seeing her and sending her away with pain in her eyes hurts me.

She tosses me a look of disgust before smirking. "I came to say Merry Christmas, jerk. I don't know how long you're in town, but I'm going out of town for a ski trip with friends."

"Aren't you too young to be going skiing?" Viv and my dad look at me like I'm nuts. She's driving me nuts in so many damn ways that I'm going to be locked up in an asylum in some hidden location for special circumstances —for men who have been tormented by little temptresses knowing exactly what they're doing. I'm both angry and hard at the same time. I could crack the damn wrench in my hand.

4

"I didn't realize there was an age limit on skiing," she hisses.

"I meant without your parents." Sometimes I just want to bend her over and spank her ass for that smart damn mouth of hers. I'm definitely getting too old for the thoughts I have of her, even though it's not entirely wrong of me. We grew up close together, but we are not family.

"Well, it's a school trip. No need to worry. The boys are staying in a different room." The smile on her face results in a deep, rigid scowl on mine. I almost crack my teeth with the way my teeth are clenched.

"Boys?" I'm about to have a mild stroke. I grip the edge of the workbench, and I hear the slightest crack. My dad taps my shoulder to remind me to let go.

"Yeah. I do go to a co-ed school, you know. Anyway, I came to say Happy Holidays. See ya." She practically skips out of the place, and my father does his best not to laugh at my fucking misery, but the damn coughing chuckle comes out.

"Come on, Son. You can finish this up and book your trip. I'll contact her daddy and get the details." Yeah, because that's what her dad wants. I can just slide on up to her vacation alone in the snowy mountains and snuggle up with his daughter where I can deflower and impregnate her. Damn, I'm getting hard thinking about it. I shake the thought from my head before I do just that to prove that she's mine.

"What? I can't go there with her." I slam my hands down on the bench, letting my head fall forward. I'm doing my best to hold it together, but I want to beat the shit out of someone. Maybe one of my Steele buddies would be up for a sparring match.

My dad grips my shoulder and asks, "Why?"

I'm defeated as I stare back at my father. "Because I don't trust myself."

He nods, understanding my dilemma. "Fine. I'll send your brothers. They could use a vacation."

"Sounds like a good deal to me." They're eighteen-year-old twins, looking for something to do. "As long as they know damn well to keep their eyes and hands where they belong."

"You know your brothers would do anything for you." Yes, they would.

I've done my best to avoid the troublemaker because when I'm around her, my heart beats out of my chest and my body reacts like every red-blooded straight male around a sexy woman like her. "Damn it. That woman is a sin."

"Sorry. If it makes you feel better, you graduate in the summer and she's legal then," he reminds me. Not damn likely.

"It's like a fucking eternity."

He taps the motorcycle we're working on and says, "Timing is everything—in motors and in love. It took me eight months to finally meet your mother."

"I guess you have a point. Not that it matters, though, because she's a minor."

"Uh-oh," he mutters.

"What is it?"

"Trouble." We're both staring at my mom.

"Clear out." I turn to the rest of the employees in my dad's shop. They all know the routine. "Hello, Mother," I greeted her with a hug.

She pulls back and gives us a mischievous grin. "So the most interesting thing happened to me today. I had the urge to go skiing for the holidays. I've already booked the entire trip to Vail."

"What?"

"Yeah. I was having lunch with Vanessa." They became close after everything that happened all those years ago. "Well, anyway. She mentioned skiing and, well, we've never been and since I have all my children here, I thought it'd be a great idea. Christmas in Vail."

"Sounds wonderful, my love."

"You're both trying to kill me."

"No. A mother knows what's good for her son. We learned that a long time ago. Besides, seventeen is legal in Texas. Although I'm not sure her father would take too kindly to his seventeen-year-old knocked up, so be smart and careful."

"I've got things to do." I shake my head and leave the garage, locking the door behind me so no one gets any kind of shock and my father doesn't have to kill anyone. I hop on my motorcycle and go for a drive.

Vail is going to be a nightmare, and I sure as fuck don't want to go. I hate skiing, and I'm not a fan of the cold, wet snow. My body shivers at the visual of having to actually participate. I'll be spending my time in the lodge or doing my best to avoid Vivian while my brothers keep track of her. There's no way I can be around her without losing my composure.

By the end of the night, I've decided that there's no way I can let her go with other men. She won't be safe with all the pricks who want between her thighs. I want between her thighs, to fill her up with my thick, long cock. The thought of sliding deep inside her slick, tight pussy stiffens me as always. Damn it. I close my eyes and grip my dick, trying to calm down. I don't need to beat off again. Almost every day I'm stroking my meat to thoughts of Vivian in so many positions.

I slam my eyes shut and groan as I recall the image of her sexy mouth sassing me today. I want to fist her hair and demand she get on her knees. She gave as good as she got, and I was being a dick. I'd show her what I thought of that spicy little mouth of hers.

"Vivian," I groan, lowering my zipper. I'm grateful that my parents gave me my own section of the house and I have a private bathroom.

Taking off my shirt, I toss it into my laundry basket and then take off my pants, sending them with my shirt. I stroll into my en-suite shower and turn it on, letting the spray get warm. When I'm fully undressed, I step in and begin soaping up, lathering my chest. With my eyes closed, those thoughts of Vivian pushed into my mind again—the way she glared, the rapid beating of her heart every time she got angry with me.

"Fuck," I groan. It raised her ample chest up and down. I want to reach out and cup those fat, round tits. Squeeze her hard nipples and pluck them, just to hear her moan for me. She would too, I could bet on it.

"Girl, you're breaking me," I grunt, imagining my lips slamming onto hers in a violent kiss that I've needed for so long. Even though Vivian is strong and independent, she's been aching for me as much as I have for her. "Knees, now," I demand after pulling her back by her long, honey-blonde hair.

"Simon," she gasps.

"You can do it, baby. You know what I want, and you want it too," I reply, guiding her to my cock that's aching for her pretty mouth. She opens up and I slide in, going as deep as she can fit. "God," I moan out, stroking the rest as she moves over my shaft. It's not long before I'm roaring my release, spraying my heavy load all over the shower wall and my hand. "Fuck." May is less than six months away. I try not to think about Viv's birthday coming up next month. The end game is graduation. Six months until we're both out of school and she'll be under me, on top of me, or even against the damn wall every fucking night. Damn, the image of pinning her to a wall is getting me hard again.

# CHAPTER TWO

## VIVIAN

WE'VE BEEN HERE LESS THAN TWO HOURS, AND I'M SO pumped to get started. I need to take a breather from my thoughts about Simon. After our confrontation at the garage, I decided that my crush on him has to come to an end. He's a grown man, and I'm a little girl in his eyes, even though we are only a few years apart.

"Vivi, are you ready?"

"Almost," I mutter, checking my reflection. I'd picked out several cute numbers online, and luckily they all arrived before we left town. There are six of us girls to a suite, and we've unpacked our suitcases and changed before heading out to meet our groups at noon in the lobby of the large hotel decked out like a fancy chalet.

I shake my head; my eyes must be playing tricks on me because I see Simon West Jr. leaning over the reception desk, chatting up the woman behind the counter. A deep rumbling chuckle comes from him as the beautiful blonde receptionist laughs at something he says, and I let out a low hiss with my fists balled low at my thighs.

*Oh, yes, it's real.* I'd know that damn laugh anywhere.

Simon West Jr. is here. I can't believe it. Why? Is he here to drive me nuts? Then I see his mom and dad. Oh, they're all here.

No one mentioned that they were planning the same vacation. No, they weren't planning it. My father did this. It's so something he would do, or rather, something my mother would set up. They never really give me any real lead before they pull on the yoke. I do my best to school my features, but there is no way to truly mask my ire. I'm so peeved that I can feel the heat spreading up my face.

"Oh my goodness, Vivian, dear. It's so good to see you," Mrs. West says, suddenly standing directly in front of me. Most of my parents' friends, I call aunt and uncle or by their patched names, but for some reason I can't with the Wests. Maybe it's the way I feel about Simon. If I treat them like family then Simon becomes family and unavailable to me and that would be awkward.

"Hello. I had no idea you'd be coming," I answer with my teeth clenched tightly together, doing my best to not scream at the way they've all invaded my peace. How *he* has invaded my peace. I can't escape the man who doesn't want me while he continues to crush my poor, fragile heart.

"Wrench told me about the trip, and I thought it would be a great way to spend a holiday with the family," Mrs. West says, smiling so sweetly that I can't be as upset as I want to be.

"That's sweet." Simon doesn't even approach. He continues speaking to the woman at the desk as if I'm nothing. I do my best not to be destroyed by it. Then, Mr. West turns his head after catching my attention. "Oh, they messed up our rooms. He's getting it settled."

"I'm sure." I smile, pretending to be unbothered. "It's good to see you all, but I'm supposed to join my group." I nod and excuse myself, walking away from them without acknowledging Simon, who is slowly moving in our direction.

"Trouble," he mutters, but I refuse to give him more than a passing nod. It's all he deserves. I've been struggling with my feelings for that man for so long. Years. I've been madly in love with him, and he's pushed me away for the last damn time. We aren't a million years apart in age, and yet, he acts like it's a crime. It's not, so it's obvious he doesn't like me and I've been wasting my damn time.

Seeing him openly flirting with another woman just confirms all the fears I had while he was in school. I've never heard or seen him with other girls in town, so this hits in a way I can't even explain. Pushing those emotions away, I head out to the ski area just off the resort to begin our first run. Thankfully I've gone skiing before, because my head isn't in the game. My heart isn't in it, either.

"Hey, pretty girl. How are you doing?" I'm so distracted I almost didn't see my classmate Richie. Luckily I stopped myself from slamming right into him.

"Hey, Richie," I say, smiling at him as best as I can. I can't truly flirt with anyone. I never could because my heart and soul have always belonged to that bastard Simon, and I'm not even sure why. He's a no-good, philandering piece of crap. I can't believe he'd be so cruel as to flirt right in front of me. He's known forever that I've been obsessed with him, and then he does that.

It's like he wants me to stop this fascination. If that's what he wants, well, that's what he'll get. From here on out, I'm not the damn doormat schoolgirl with a crush on the hunky mechanic. God, it's not like I haven't been warned by him several times to go home and grow up. Well, now I'm done being the pathetic little simpering Vivian who wears her heart on her sleeve.

"Things are going better now that you're here."

"That's what I'm talking about. Do you want to be my partner for the day?" he asks.

"Sure, I'd like that," I say, smiling at him while walking toward the ski instructor. I see Simon's nosy brothers nearby and roll my eyes. If I could get away with it, I'd kick them in their shins, but then I wouldn't doubt that they'd accidentally trip me in the snow. Unfortunately, we've grown up way too close to each other, and it's like having extra brothers.

"Come on, Richie. Let's go over here." I move him away from the twins so I don't have to deal with their pestering.

Over the past two years, I've gotten used to their big-brother antics, but they aren't *my* big brothers, so they can quit it.

"So, are you seeing anyone?" he asks, his intent clear.

"Yeah," twin one asks, stepping around me. Where the hell did he come from? How did I not hear him crunch through the snow?

The other pops his head over Richie's shoulder and says, "Yes, she's seeing a therapist because she's in love with my brother and she doesn't understand that she's jailbait."

Number one rests his arm on my shoulder and shakes his head. "One more month and she's fair game for Simon, but she's too damn impatient. Girls," he sighs.

"I think you boys are full of shit because she's clearly here with me," Richie tells them. I smirk.

"He's right," I say.

"We gave you a warning, Richie, but you're just a placeholder. I hate to say it, but once my brother finds out, you'll be the last placeholder for anyone."

I want to punch both of them, but instead, I think it would be better to prove them wrong. I grab Richie by his snow vest and pull him in close, but before I can lock lips with him, he suddenly slips on his skis. I feel so bad.

"Dude, what a bad look," Jackass number two says, annoying me so much I clock him in the jaw. He takes it with a smile, stumbling back in the snow.

"Seriously, could you be more of a prick?" I screech.

"I could. Is that a challenge?"

"Ugh," I huff and leave all three of them there because even though Richie fell, he isn't hurt and all he wanted from me was to keep him warm this weekend—something that is not going to happen.

I ride the slopes for a few hours with a couple of the girls, avoiding all the neanderthals because the only one I want isn't anywhere to be found.

He's probably inside keeping himself well occupied with all the snow bunnies and their personal attention. I do my best to hold back the pain that bubbles in my chest.

"Are you okay, Ms. Lawrence?"

I turn to my instructor, who is a handsome thirty-something-year-old man who has ladies flocking to him with his charming smile, but I'm not one of them. "Um. Yes."

"Whoever he is, don't let him bring you down. You're young and beautiful. One day when you grow up, you'll meet the right man." I want to scream. What the hell is it with the whole growing-up BS? Yes, I'm freaking young, and I know it, but still, I'm my parents' child, so I'm also stubborn and determined.

I may not be an adult, but my mother was just as young as me and so was Simon's mother. If Simon's brothers were being legit, he's just waiting for me to grow up, but he's not really waiting, is he? More like enjoying his time while I wait. He was having a free-for-all with all the ladies—a full buffet of women at his disposal and in his bed while I long for him.

"Thank you. I promise I'm fine. I'm done for today and am going to return to the resort and to my room."

I manage to return to the resort, checking in with my group so they don't panic, and then go to my room without running into another damn West family member. Then, I give a quick call to my parents before showering the chill off my body. Once I'm good, I get some sleep because I'm worn out.

I'm woken up a few hours later by my roommates. "Girl, what are you doing sleeping in? Dang. Was it too much?"

"Did you take all those boys at once?"

"What?" Are they assuming that I was screwing a bunch of guys?

"You were with all those guys."

"Are you three serious? I wasn't with anyone. Seriously. Two of them are like annoying brothers, and Richie and I are friends." I roll my eyes. "What would make you think that? Since when is talking to some of the guys in school mean I'm having sex with them?"

"Richie said you hooked up."

"Richie's a fucking liar." Ugh. When I see him tomorrow, I'm going to kick him in his sack. I can't believe he would go so far as to make up some crap like that.

# CHAPTER THREE

## SIMON

AFTER OUR TEPID GREETING YESTERDAY, I KNOW THAT VIVIAN won't be too keen on seeing me this morning, so I keep my distance. My brothers did their job, low-key following her and her classmates around the slopes. Since they were with the group, they all knew my brothers and had wanted to hang with them, which annoyed Vivian.

I stay in the lodge, hating skiing more than I hate snow. With a hot cup of coffee, I open a book and sit on one of the cozy sofas to enjoy the nice silence. It doesn't last long when a snow bunny appears in all her tight gear, bringing the chill in with her. Snow falls from her right at my feet and onto my book. I shake it off my book before it's ruined and then lie the book flat on the sofa so it can dry. If it's ruined, I'm going to be pissed.

Looking up, I say, "Excuse me." My tone isn't polite, but from the look on her face, I'm sure she doesn't get it.

"Oh, I didn't mean to get in your way," she says with a giggle, as if attempting to be cute, but it's not working for me. I just want her out of my way. I stand up, but she doesn't move far enough, so when I reach my full height, we're mere inches from each other.

"I see why you can't make it onto the slopes, West," Trouble says, smirking at me with her arms crossed.

"Ooh, we were just getting to know each other," the snow bunny teases Trouble. I roll my eyes because I haven't done anything wrong, while she spent the day yesterday surrounded by other men, flirting and chatting it up.

I'd gotten message after message from my brothers. There had been a guy my woman was hanging around with all day. They even had to stop them from kissing. I could smash his face in. My brain throbs as I consider how close things came between her and someone else.

What the hell am I supposed to do about that little prick? I know what the fuck I want to do, but killing that asshole is against the law and someone would link it to me for sure because there are too many witnesses seeing them together.

"I didn't mean to interrupt. I'm not interested in anything he has to offer. I just want you to tell your attack dogs to back off. Just because I'm not old enough for you doesn't mean I'm not old enough for boys my age." She moves past before I can grab at her arm, and the damn bimbo gets in my way.

"Well, it looks like she won't be a problem."

"Look, I'm not sure where you got the idea that I want anything to do with you, but I don't."

"I thought we had a connection."

"What? Have we even met?"

"I worked at the desk yesterday." Oh. Did she think I was flirting with her? Holy hell. I was thinking about the conversation.

*"So Miss…um…Sarah."*

*"Yes," she says. "How can I help you?"*

*"Um…my mother ordered our rooms and there's been some mix-up."*

*"Oh, goodness. Let me get that straightened out. What's the name?"*

*"Simon West."*

*"I like that name, but I'm going to need the name on the account."*

*"That's what it's booked under."*

*"Oh, I thought you were giving me yours," she giggles.*

*"Well, it's my name as well. I'm named after my father."*

*"Oh, this explains the mix-up here. Someone assumed from the name that it was double booked and canceled the room. I'm sorry about that. We can get you a new room, but unfortunately it's on the opposite side of the resort where the school kids are at,"* she sighs.

*"Are you serious?" I scowl.*

*"I'm sorry, sir, but…oh shit, my boss is coming. I'm going to get fired for this mix-up."*

*I start laughing and tap my ID on the counter. "I'll have to take that last room. I should have booked sooner. Thanks for taking care of it," I say, winking at her. As shitty as the problem is, I don't want the girl to get fired.*

I shake my head. "I'm sorry, but I was just trying to let you keep your job. I don't want anything to do with you."

"Well, that girl is still a girl, obviously, and too young for you. I'm your age."

"Nothing about you is relevant. Besides, she lives in my town, and I've been in love with her for years, so mind your fucking business." I storm away back to my room, annoyed by the fucking girl whose name I couldn't remember.

I toss the book on my bed and punch the damn door. That woman messed up my relationship. No, I messed it up, but she added the fucking final nail in the coffin. Damn it. I don't know how to fix it when I only have months to go.

There's a knock at my door, and it's my mother. "What's up, Mom?" I ask as I open it, giving her room to enter. She steps inside and closes the door behind her.

"We're going to dinner at the restaurant next to the hotel, sweetie. Are you going to join us?"

"I'll be down shortly."

"Good. Things will get better with Vivian. You're only a

few months away, and you can still work out the misunderstandings."

"Thanks. We'll see."

I jump in the shower, and I step out with a towel wrapped around my waist. I nearly fall back on my ass when I see the girl from the lobby there. "What the fuck?"

"Sorry, I thought you could use some towels." She looks down at my towel and gasps. I wish I'd beaten off in the shower, but then she would have heard or seen me since she felt the need to just walk in.

"Since when are you part of housekeeping?" I question through my clenched teeth.

"Damn. You don't have to be rude, but I can't see why you're all hung up on her when you're packing all that for a girl who is out there flirting with all the little boys, and there are grown women who would handle you just right."

"Get the fuck out of my room before I throw you out," I roar. She drops the towels on the bed, and that's when I notice that her top buttons are undone. "What the fuck kind of game are you playing? I'm going to call your damn boss. Get out, now, or I'll have you fired. Don't even think of trying to claim any assault bullshit, either. My mother was just in here, and she's expecting me for dinner."

She gasps, then quickly rushes to the door but slowly exits it, closing it to look like she wasn't kicked out. Fucking cunt. I'm on the phone to the main desk right away. "I need to speak to the hotel manager immediately."

"Yes, sir." The man on the call transfers the line.

It rings several times before I'm forced to leave a message for Mr. Steiner. "Hello, my name is Simon West Jr., and I'm calling because I was accosted by one of your employees. She entered my hotel room tonight while I was in the shower. She came with towels, even though she isn't a housekeeper. After I asked her why, she made sexual advances with her top unbuttoned. I sent her away with the promise of calling you. I don't remember her name... I believe it's Susan, Sandra, Sarah, something like that." I end the call when my phone buzzes.

> Damn, bro. I never expected that from you.

It's a text from Eric that includes a picture, and it's the chick that just left my room as she's buttoning her top outside my door. *Fuck.*

*It's not what you think. I didn't do shit with her and kicked her out of my room.*

*Well, it didn't look like that, and I'm not the only one who saw it.*

*God, please tell me it wasn't Viv.*

*Sorry, bro.*

I'm running my hand through my hair just as someone knocks at my fucking door again. Damn it, it's probably my brother, so I go to open it and it's Vivian, looking shocked and heart-fucking-broken. I grip her wrist as she tries to run away.

"Get the fuck in here," I say, pulling her into the room and slamming the door shut.

"No, you bastard." She reaches out to slap me, but I'm quick enough to grab her hand and I slam her back against the wooden surface.

"Don't tell me no after you come in here. You want to fight? We're going to have it out, Trouble."

"Simon, your towel. It fell," she gasps.

"Yes, it did."

"You're naked," she pants as my dick throbs between my legs, nearly pressing against her sweet cunt, but I hold back.

"Then I suggest you don't look down, baby, because you're going to get a sneak preview of what you will get in five months when you graduate." She looks down despite herself. "If you keep pushing me, you might get it next month for your birthday."

Her eyes widen and her mouth opens, causing my cock to jerk with arousal. "Oh my goodness."

"I warned you, but you can't help yourself." Unable to resist, I firmly grind my cock against her tiny mound, letting her feel what she fucking does to me. "This is only for you."

She scoffs, rolling her eyes at me.

I grip her chin firmly. "I didn't fuck the bitch that I just kicked out of my room."

"Then why was she in here, and why are you only in a towel?"

I grip her hair and slam her head back while I stare into her gorgeous, greenish-brown eyes. "Because she's trying to get laid, and I was in the damn shower, trying to fight off the need to beat off to images of you on your knees for me." I rock my hips upward, jutting my cock along her split, and watch her shiver.

"I would never."

"Don't lie, Vivian. One day, I'll have that pretty, vicious tongue doing swirls around this fat cock before I bury it deep in your pussy." I know I'm pushing our boundaries, dropping the damn barrier between us until there is nothing left.

"Simon." Her voice falters as she whimpers out my name with her eyes closed and lips parted. Unable to miss the opportunity, I lay my lips on hers, tasting her sweet kiss.

"Viv," I moan around her mouth. "Fuck, we can't do this. This isn't right. You need to leave—now." I force myself to push away before I toss her on the bed and fuck my kid into her untouched womb. It shouldn't be a big deal because her father knows damn well that I plan to knock her up the second we both graduate. There's no doubt in my mind that is what's going to happen.

"You're the one completely naked, holding me here. Didn't you get enough from your last chick?"

"I told you, I didn't fuck her, and I didn't invite her into my room. Stop being so damn jealous when there is no one for me but you."

"She saw you like this?"

"No. I had the towel on, baby."

"Well, it's not like it makes much of a difference. There's no way to hide anything under there."

"What the fuck do you want me to do, Vivian? It's not like I could have stopped her from coming in here."

"No, but if you wouldn't have been flirting with every blonde with big tits, then they wouldn't throw themselves at you."

"Is that why you throw yourself at me?" I regret the words the second they leave my lips, but it's already too late.

"God, I'm sorry that I have. You've corrected that problem. You have one less big-breasted blonde after you now." She gives me a shove, just enough to create space, and leaves my room. I'd chase after her ass, but I'm still naked. Damn it.

Dressing as fast as I can, I head out into the lobby with my coat and hat in hand because I need to meet my parents, and taking Vivian's bratty ass sounds like a great idea.

Right now, I could use my parents' help. I fucked things up so damn bad, but I'm not sure how the hell I'm supposed to fix it. I need to find her and straighten shit out before I lose the love of my life. There is no way I want her thinking I was fucking that scheming whore or anyone else.

I hit the lobby, and it's my worst nightmare come to life. Vivian is with some guy, smiling, and I'm filled with pure possessive rage. This asshole is trying to put the moves on Vivian. This trip has been one hellish moment after another, but this has to take the fucking cake. She doesn't bother to shoo his ass away. No, she continues talking to him as if he hasn't tried to slide his hand onto her waist more than once. I want to rip his heart out like mine is, but it's not his fault that Vivian is beautiful and single.

No, that's mine, and I know that I've antagonized her, made her think that I didn't care, pushed her away to keep my lust at bay, but damn it, can't she see how much I'm obsessed with her? Hell, it doesn't help that she saw that bitch come out of my room half-dressed, and my foolish, lust-filled attempt to correct myself blew up in my face.

When he brushes her hair out of the way, I lose my temper. Having enough, I storm up to them.

"What the fuck, Vivian?" I snap, glaring at her. She doesn't flinch one bit, but her pretty hazel eyes are full of emotion.

"Oh, I didn't see you there, Simon," she says, smiling up at me while still standing extremely close to this prick, inviting his touch as if intentionally torturing me.

"Obviously you didn't because you wouldn't have been flirting with this asshole, unless you want me to break his face and fingers," I snarl, giving him a cold, warning glance. I swear I've seen him around town, and he should know better than to touch my woman.

"Whoa. I'm not trying to overstep." He throws his hands up and quickly walks away, not even daring to give

Vivian a second glance. She thought she had a tough guy there, but the pussy was quick to bow out, which was wise.

She's so damn adorable when she's pissed. I want to take her back to my room and finish what we started by bending her over my knee, pulling down those tight fucking pants, and reddening her ass until she calms the fuck down, but that's not going to happen for several months. "How dare you, Simon? For three years, I've given you my undivided attention and adoration, only for you to continue to act as if I'm bothering you. Don't come over here trying to act like you're entitled to tell me who I can and can't talk to."

"Entitled? You're out of your damn mind. Just because you're pissed at me doesn't mean you get to flirt with all these stupid, eager dicks out here. I'm trying to stop both of you from making a stupid decision."

"Stupid decision? You got snow bunnies jumping in your lap and out of your damn bed. You're screwing every blonde while demanding I behave. I thought I made it clear that I was no longer on the long list of many admirers. So, Mr. West, I am allowed to date whoever the fuck I want…and that doesn't include you."

"You're making a big mistake, Vivian." I grip her by her wrist, feeling the way her pulse upticks.

"No, I made a mistake falling for you." She looks over my shoulder to a group of girls. "I have people waiting for me. Oh, and one of them is an admirer of yours too," she adds with a scoff. She's pointing at Shelby Colman. Her father's a great customer of mine, but she doesn't know how to take the hint that I have no interest in her.

My phone rings in my pocket. It's my dad, who is probably wondering where I am, but I send it to voicemail. "Take your call and leave me alone. In fact, I hope we never see each other again. Forget you ever knew me, and I'll do the same."

God, I'm so fucking aroused and pissed at the same time. She's the only damn blonde with big tits that I want, but she has no damn idea how hard it is to deny myself. I want to pull her into my arms to kiss her, and also yell at her to see the truth.

Instead, I take a calming breath and behave like a responsible adult. "Fine, but don't go doing anything we'll both regret and can't take back." I storm away before I do something I will regret.

"Don't worry—we won't see each other again to feel that regret." What the fuck is that supposed to mean?

I reach out and pull her back to me so her chest slams into mine. "Tell me what the hell that's supposed to mean, Vivian."

"It means I have no intention of waiting around for a fucker who plays the field."

"We aren't having this discussion here. Let's go somewhere…"

Before I can drag her away from the crowded lounge, a man comes between us. I know the fucker because he was my teacher at one point. "Do we have a problem, Ms.

Lawrence?"

"No, Mr. Hart. Mr. West was just leaving." She gives me a snarky smirk.

I've never felt so pissed off in my life. How could she say such bullshit? Does she think I'm out here chasing women? I only came on this trip because my parents wanted me here. If I'd come on my own, I wouldn't have stopped until she and I were in bed together.

Filled with rage, I slip on my coat, hat, and gloves, and leave the resort. This isn't over between us, but now isn't the time to get shit straight.

Instead of turning toward the restaurant, I shoot a text to my dad.

> Sorry, I can't make dinner. Other plans.

Everything okay?

> I just need some air.

Just be careful, Son. We love you.

> I love you all too.

The snowfall is light as I head down the road, and it's not as cold as I expected, or maybe it's my damn temper keeping me warm. Either way, I march down the street, using the lamps to light my way.

I haven't heard from the manager yet, but then again, it's late and maybe my concern isn't that damn important.

Either way, I'm going to be gone soon, and as long as that bitch stays away from me, I'll be fine.

I've walked for about two hours, the cold seeping through my bones. I'm about to head back to the hotel when I see bright lights shining in my face. It's that fucking bitch from the hotel and some other woman I've never met. They fly down the road, passing me by. When they spot me, they slam on their brakes, skidding in the snow.

They reverse, coming to a stop next to me. "Mr. West, what are you doing out in the snow?"

"Taking a walk." I have my phone out for safety precautions. I'm about to redial my father's number. I don't trust these two. Well, most of all this woman.

"I hope you don't freeze out here. We could give you a ride," the other girl offers.

"No, he's not interested. He reported me to the boss, but fortunately, he's my daddy so nothing is going to happen. Still, I'm willing to forgive him and warm him up." She winks at me.

"Go away."

"Gosh, you probably aren't packing anyway," her friend says.

"Oh, he is." She wags her brows, and I want to crush her. It's because of her that Vivian and I are even at odds to begin with. Our relationship had been on the edge of insanity as it was. All I needed was some asshole to tip us over, and that bitch had to be the one.

"You're both pathetic. Leave me alone before I destroy you." I roll my fucking eyes and continue walking back to the hotel. I'm checking out by morning. My parents can either come with me or celebrate Christmas without me. I'm done. I trudge through the snowy pass, taking the route back to the hotel through the lit streets.

It takes so long that I'm damn near frozen. I didn't realize how long I've been out here, but at least I'm pretty close to the resort entrance. Suddenly I hear the sound of tires in the snow. When I turn my head, I can't get out of the way fast enough, and the metal hits my body and the world goes dark. *Goodbye, Trouble.*

# CHAPTER FOUR

## VIVIAN

"Girl, did you and that monkey wrench finally do it like animals?"

"What?"

"Come on—don't deny it. You have a mark on your neck, and he was so dang possessive of you in the hall," Shelby continues.

"Ms. Colman, please keep your conversations down. We don't need to know about Ms. Lawrence's relationship with Mr. West."

"It's okay, Mr. Hart. Shelby's just jealous because she's been trying to get her hands on someone like Simon and it hasn't worked," Quinn says, sticking her tongue out at Shelby who flips her off.

"Enough, girls." Mr. Hart rubs between his brows in frustration. I receive glares from Shelby for the rest of dinner, but I ignore them because my mind is on Simon. I've been thinking about what he said. Even though he was a jerk, I want to talk to him and maybe figure this thing out between us.

"Where's Richie?" I ask Quinn in a hushed voice, hoping that bitch Shelby didn't hear me.

"Why? Looking for another fucking lay?" Shelby hisses.

"He said he wasn't feeling well and stayed back at the hotel," Quinn says. She rolls her eyes at Shelby who sticks her tongue out at Quinn.

Funny, when I saw Richie earlier, he was fine. Maybe it was the encounter with Simon that upset him. He has that effect on people—ruining plans is his thing.

My plans for the future aren't set in stone, and they sure as hell aren't solely based on Simon. The way he said that I was his makes me believe he's been telling me the truth. A part of me needs to know more. When we return to the resort, I pretend to go to my room, but instead, I stroll toward Simon's room. I pace back and forth outside of his door after coming back from dinner with my classmates. I'm still thinking about the way his mouth was on mine and the dirty promises that he made to me about our future.

I paced outside his door when he doesn't answer for at least twenty minutes. I'm about to leave when his parents come down the hall with his brothers and sister. "Is Simon inside?" his mother asks.

"No. In fact, I was waiting for him to come back."

"Come back?"

"Yes. We had a fight and he stormed off, and I left with my class to dinner."

"He didn't come back in all that time?"

"No. At least, not that I'm aware of."

"Oh my God." Mrs. West looks at her husband. "Simon. My baby. Where is he?" she sobs.

Simon's brother Eric comes up to me and says, "We didn't get to talk earlier, but I wanted to show you something —"

He's about to tell me when Simon's dad says, "He's not answering his phone."

The sound of sirens can be heard in the distance. Mrs. West places a hand on her belly; panic is etched on her face. "Calm down, Dash. Our boy is okay. There's always someone getting hurt on the slopes or out drunk. Simon is probably at the bar or gone to get some food. Maybe his phone is out of battery."

A classmate of mine comes running in. "Mr. and Mrs. West. It's your son." He tries to catch his breath and then continues, "It's Simon. He was hit by a car. They are taking him to the hospital right now."

"Oh my God." I can't hear anything as the room spins and goes dark.

I'M WOKEN UP BY ERIC, WHO WIPES A TOWEL OVER MY FACE. "Viv, you're awake. Thank goodness. We're so glad that you're okay." I look around, and I'm on the sofa in the middle of the hotel luxury lounge with Simon's siblings.

"Who cares about me? What is going on with Simon?" I question.

"He's in surgery, and we don't know what's going on."

"What about your mom? Is she okay?" I can't imagine being in her position. My heart is breaking for both of us.

"She's with my dad right now. They are in the OR waiting room." I look around and see all of his siblings staring at me with so much worry when they should be at the hospital with their parents and their brother.

"Why aren't you all there?"

"Dad wanted us to wait here and get ready to check out in case we need to move to the hotel next to the hospital," Eric answers.

"Oh."

"Here, drink this," his sister, Abby, offers, handing me a bottle of water.

"We have everything packed," Jack says, taking a seat on the sofa across from me. "So we are ready to go to the hospital."

"Oh my God. Who would be that stupid to be walking out in this bad weather in the first place?" we overhear someone say. My fists are balled up in anger at the person with a big mouth.

Someone else adds, "It's not stupid. It's a fucking ski resort. It's cold everywhere—duh. Besides, maybe the asshole who was driving should have been more careful. It was a hit and run. Still, it's lucky that Sarah found him and got an ambulance before it was too late."

I try not to cry because he left angry at me, and he wouldn't have been outside if it wasn't for me. "Excuse me, but I need to call my parents," I say. I gently attempt to push off the sofa, but Abby shakes her head and grips my shoulder, holding me down.

"I already did," Jack says.

"Thanks. What did they say?"

"They will be here tomorrow," he says.

I'm out of my seat, standing in shock. I can't believe that they're rushing here because I fainted. "They don't need to do that. The trip finishes tomorrow and I'm fine, anyway."

"You're not going to stay?" Abby asks.

"I didn't think anyone wanted me here," I confess.

"Girl, I told you that my brother wasn't kidding about his feelings."

"But I'm the reason he was outside."

"Did you hit him with the car?" Abby asks me with her hands on her hips.

"No, of course not," I gasp.

"Then he should have come to dinner with us like he was supposed to instead of sulking like he's been doing for days," Abby replies, taking my hand in hers. "He didn't want to be here in the first place, and Mom made him come here because she wanted us together for the holidays. Still, whoever hit him is to blame, and no one else. Understand?"

"Yes," I say, even though I'm not sure it's that easy to believe it.

Jack takes a call from their parents, and we wait for their conversation to end to learn the news. "He's still in surgery, but they said to sleep until we have more news. They aren't leaving. Mom has been given a room at the hospital because Dad wasn't going to take no for an answer."

I start heading toward my suite, but I'm suddenly lifted off my feet and cradled by Jack. "Nope. We're on strict orders to bring you back to our suite. You can have our parents' room for the night. We need to make sure you're okay." I start crying, clinging to Jack.

"Already moving onto the next brother," Sarah mutters as we pass her. That woman is worse than Shelby. At least Shelby actually knows Simon is a great guy and wants him for more than the fact that he's hot.

"Since you called the ambulance, I'm going to let you keep breathing out of that fake nose of yours," Abby says.

"Don't be so hostile. It's not like we can't get along. Simon and I were having such a great night together. After our dinner, we took a long walk and were almost back when that idiot jumped onto the sidewalk and Simon pushed me out of the way. He's always a gentleman." She winks at me before sauntering off.

Deep down in my heart I know she's lying, but the pain is so real and fresh that I want to scream. She's the cause of all this, and I hate her from the depths of my soul. Why was she around to help Simon? Did she have something to do with his accident, or was she still trying to seduce him?

Jack refuses to let me get away, and with a swiftness I don't expect, he picks me up again and carries me away. "Just rest. Simon will be okay. He's strong, and we need to be strong for him." They bring me into the suite, and Jack lays me down on the bed, kissing my forehead before covering me with the blanket.

"Good night, little sister," he whispers, closing the door behind him. I close my eyes and dream about Simon.

---

MY OWN SCREAMS STARTLE ME AWAKE. I SIT UP WITH MY hand pressed to my heart, breathing heavily. This trip was a mistake, and I wish I could do it over again. There is a note from the family saying my parents are here, and that they went to the hospital to see their brother. I leave the suite and go to mine to change. After I'm dressed, I go looking for my parents in the main lobby area.

"Honey, there you are." My mother drags me into her arms, hugging me with a frantic urgency that scares me. I hope they don't tell me that he died.

"I'm sorry, sweetie. We got here as soon as we could. We spoke to Wrench this morning. Simon is in a coma. The doctor is really worried that he might not make it, but this is good because at least he has a chance. They believe it's only temporary."

I collapsed, knees buckled, unable to breathe. I shouldn't have said what I said. I can't believe my last words were full of anger just because I was jealous. My father picks me up off the floor, scooping me in his arms and carrying me to the sofa—the same sofa I saw Simon standing by the other day. "We're going to go there right now, okay, kiddo?"

"Daddy, he has to be okay," I sob. My words are barely audible through the tears. I know we will never be together, but that doesn't mean I want him to be hurt.

"He's going to make it. He's too strong. Too pig-headed to just give up."

"I hope so," I cry. My mother runs her hand through my hair.

"Sweetheart, we're going to warm up the car," my father says, standing up and then leaving. My mother takes his place, hugging me tightly.

"I wish we never came on this stupid vacation."

"We know."

Her phone rings, and she answers it. "It's time to go, Vivian, dear." We get up, and my legs are so weak I barely can stand. Still, I have to see Simon.

"Dad, I just want to lie down," I mutter as I slide into the back seat. "We'll wake you up when we get to the hospital," my father says.

"Simon, why? Why?" I quietly whimper as I lay my head on the leather seat. My heart aches and I cry myself to sleep, waking several times to cry some more until my throat is hoarse and completely dry.

He has been airlifted to a hospital in Salt Lake City, so the drive was much longer than expected. It's not until the middle of the evening that my parents wake me up. My heart ends up in my throat.

"Can I see him?" I beg, looking messy but I don't care.

"Yes, we're going to take you inside the hospital right now."

When they do, I'm completely devastated, and the sight is nearly unbearable. He's hooked to so many machines that are monitoring him, and he's covered in so many bandages that I can hardly tell that's him. His handsome face is swollen, and I can't look away from his broken hand. The hands that love working on vehicles. I hope that he not only pulls through, but he can continue to do what he loves.

"We're going to get some rooms. You can stay for a while, Vivian, dear," my dad says, kissing my forehead before leaving the room.

Mrs. West squeezes my hand and says, "I know what that woman said to you, but you have to know it's not true."

"Why was she there?"

"We'll see." She lets go and wipes her tears.

"Come on, Dash. We need you to sit down and rest." Mr. West is extremely protective of his family.

There is a knock at the door, and then the doctor comes in. "Excuse me, but there are too many people in this room. I'm sorry, but some of you must wait outside."

"We understand," Jack says. I get up to leave, and then he shakes his head. "Stay a few minutes." They all leave, giving me a moment alone with Simon.

I look at the man I've loved for so long. "I'm sorry. I regret everything I said, and I hope they're right and you didn't go out with that woman last night, but I can't say I blame you after everything. Please just get better." I lean down and kiss his cheek, and then wipe my tears before walking out of the room.

Eric stops me. "Hey, there's something I want to show you, and I keep getting stopped. You need to see this. Regardless of what happens, you need to see this." He hands me his phone, and I read through the conversation between Simon and him. He reported that bitch, so he most definitely wouldn't have gone out with her. I knew he was telling me the truth in the room, but it doesn't matter right now.

"She's lying," Eric says. He grips my shoulder and looks me in the eye. "My brother loves you, and I know you love him. I'm hoping he pulls through because you two have to get your shit together. You are perfect for each other. Two damn dummies." He pulls me in for a hug.

"Thank you, Eric."

"You're welcome, brat. Now, go and eat some food."

---

THE NEXT FEW DAYS FEEL LIKE A NIGHTMARE. EVERYTHING and everyone are chaotic. No one has answers to who drove the vehicle that hit Simon, and he isn't doing any better. He has moments of going up and down and it's so scary. Still, I sit at the hospital waiting and hoping just like everyone else.

"Sheriff, it's not like that," I whip my head around in the hospital lobby to find that bitch from the hotel. I want to rush up and slap her in the face, but she's speaking to two officers, Mr. and Mrs. West.

"If you keep making that face it's going to stay that way," my mother whispers conspiratorially at my side.

"What face?"

"Like she'd be dead if no one was around." I hadn't realized the violent rage was showing on my face.

"Oops."

Moments later the police escort the bitch away and Mr. and Mrs. West come to our side. "How are you doing, Viv?" Mrs. West asks as she gently squeezes my elbow.

"I'm fine," I muttered.

A deep, rumbling chuckle comes from Mr. West that reminds me so much of Simon that I'm taken aback by the sound. "Sorry, that was the biggest bullshitting I'm fine I've heard today."

"Leave her alone. I'd like to rip that girl's hair out too," she says.

"I remember when that was me," my mom remarks.

"Goodness, you were never that bad."

"I think back then you would have disagreed."

"No, that girl claimed to have been with Simon when he got hit. Now she said that she only said that to start some drama. She just happened to be out when she spotted him."

"Are you serious?"

"Yes, so she doesn't know who hit him?"

"No," Mr. West says.

"I bet she only said those things to make Vivian jealous," Mrs. West added.

"I want to rip her hair out myself," my mother says. I pace around the waiting room lobby.

I drop down to one of the less than comfortable chairs, letting my mind wander as our parents talk. Slowly, I tune in to their conversation. "Well, I think we should go back to the hotel and get some well needed sleep. We don't have any answers and it's getting late. We'll be here first thing in the morning."

"It's a good idea. We all need it."

"When is Law coming back?"

"Tomorrow," my mom answers Mr. West.

"Good, you both need the support. I would say to take her home, but I know that's just not going to happen."

"It's like telling me to leave Law or Dash to leave your side."

"You're damn right."

My mother taps my arm, and I absently look up at her. "Sorry, sweetie, but we should get back to the hotel and rest."

"Okay. I heard, and my eyes are starting to feel heavy." Nothing is heavier than my heart, but until Simon is better, I'll be in this miserable state. I head into my temporary bedroom and strip out of my clothes, showering away the day at the hospital before snuggling under the covers. Hopefully tomorrow is a better day and Simon gives us a sign he's on the mend.

# CHAPTER FIVE

## SIMON

A STEADY BEEPING SOUND, GROWING SLOWLY, PLAYS IN MY ears. It makes my head pound, and I lift my hand to rub my temple, causing a pain to shoot through my arm. I let out a roar.

The beeping intensifies, and then I hear footsteps approaching. My eyes open, but the light is blinding.

"Hello, Simon. Do you know where you are?" a voice calls out. It sounds distant, vague, and my head throbs, but I have no idea who it is or where it's coming from.

I open my eyes several times and get a better look at my surroundings.

"It looks…" I try to clear my throat, but it's so dry that I start coughing. I rub my hand over my mouth and then cup my throat. My hand is attached to an IV, so I must be in the hospital, but for how long and why is a mystery. I close my eyes and lay my head against the pillow. The softness behind my head can't dull the ache in my skull. *What the hell is going on?* It is killing me.

"I'm sorry. Let me get you some water." She leaves, and I'm left confused. I can't remember how I ended up in the hospital. Everything is a blur, and all I can recall is the cold snow. I try to think back to what happened, but nothing is coming to mind.

The woman doesn't take long to return, and when she does, the sound of her voice annoys me. "I'm back," she says cheerfully, like I'm supposed to be happy about it. I'm not sure why I'm feeling rude, but her tone is too light for me. Maybe it's because my head is pounding out of control or something, but I'm not in the mood, or maybe I'm just an asshole. "Your family will be called in to see you soon."

"Family?"

"Yes, you were on vacation with them."

"Where are they?" I ask.

"They were sent back to the hotel. It's three in the morning, but we can call and leave them a message," she says.

"Where am I?" I question, finding my voice that feels rough with every word.

"You're at the hospital in Salt Lake City, Utah."

"Utah?"

"Yes. Do you not remember how you got here? You were airlifted from Vail, Colorado."

"No, I don't. The last thing I remember was working at an auto body shop." I lie to her because there is a lot that's flashing through my head way too fast. So many memories and people, but they don't make any sense. I don't know who anyone is, but one memory becomes very clear. A woman is yelling at me, but I recognize her so well. She's so damn beautiful that her words cut like a knife to my chest, and the pain makes my head hurt some more.

"The doctor will be in to see you and can explain more. Oh my goodness, your blood pressure is spiking and your heart rate is jumping." She presses the emergency buttons before shooting something into my IV, and then I slowly feel my eyes growing heavy again.

I don't know how long I've been out, but when I wake up, all the memories are gone; those violent flashes were pushed to the side.

There is a light knock on the door, and then a man enters. Given his attire, I can only assume he's a doctor. "Mr. West, it's a great start to the New Year. I'm Dr. Hart, your primary physician. Your family will be so relieved." New Year? What the hell?

"Doc, how did I get here?" I question.

"You were in a serious accident."

Vail is meant for the slopes, and I'm not a snow guy. I've never skied in my life. "I didn't go skiing; I don't like skiing," I mutter, shaking my head, and I stop abruptly because it's painful.

"No, you were injured in a car accident; a drunk driver hit you." I have no recollection of the incident, and it must show on my face because he continues. "You were walking back to the hotel when you were struck. Your injuries are severe, but thankfully the cold helped with the swelling and we got to you when we did. You're lucky to be alive. I need to check your vitals, and then we're going to let you sleep."

He flashes a light in my eyes, checking them, and then nods. "First, let me ask: do you know your name?"

"Yes, Simon West, Jr.," I answer with an impatient sigh.

"That's good. I'm sorry that my questions seem basic and redundant, Simon."

"Is that really good? I'm missing time. I'm in a completely different state, and I'm not sure how the hell I got here." A wave of panic fills me, and I want to jump out of bed. How much time have I lost?

He looks at the machines beside me and says, "Calm down, Mr. West. It's very common, given your injuries. The nurse did say your last memory is your family's auto body shop and you know you don't like skiing, so more than likely this is a temporary situation. Please rest and calm yourself. The memories will come in time. We will run some tests to be sure that there are no lasting effects, but I'm certain it's just a little hiccup in your recovery."

"You have got to be kidding me. A little hiccup?"

"Simon, there could be worse things to happen. You have only been in a coma for a week. Most people in your situation have a lot more problems."

"How about those meds now, Doc?" I'm not in the mood for his positive thinking. Did he just tell me I was in a coma for a week? I've been out of it for a week and don't remember how I got to Vail in the first place. I knew we were going, but I'm missing a good chunk of time. I close my eyes and ponder how bad it could have been. Hell, what happened to me?

The door to the room burst open. "Oh my God, he's awake," my mother says with a cheerful sob. "My baby," she coos, coming up to my bedside and giving me the lightest squeeze.

"Dash, be careful, love." My father's deep voice, although stern, has always carried a sweet and gentle tone for my mother. Several others enter the room, but the one who draws my attention is the same woman who yelled at me in my hazy state. It takes me a moment to realize that it's none other than Vivian—or Trouble, as I like to call her. Her eyes are red rimmed, like she's been crying for days, and she doesn't look well.

"Excuse me, but you all can't be in here. Mr. West is about to get some rest and go for testing."

"Rest? The man has been sleeping for two weeks," Eric says.

"It's not the same thing as true rest. Besides, we have some important matters to discuss with Mr. and Mrs. West."

"What he wants to say is that I don't remember anything since we left Steeleville. I don't know what happened to me or why I was outside." I look straight at my pretty little beauty, hating that I don't remember this trip. She stares at me with tears in her eyes, mouth gaping widely until her hand covers it. Somehow, I hate that I'm hurting her by not remembering the reason for our fight, but I don't. All I can remember is the bitterness in her tone as she wished she'd never see me again.

Vivian's phone rings, and she says, "Oops. It's just my parents. They probably want an update. Excuse me." She leaves the room, and it suddenly feels colder, emptier without her in it.

Even if her phone didn't ring, I knew she wanted to leave. Without Vivian here, there is no reason for me to be awake right now. "I've got a headache, and I'm tired."

"We're going to leave and let you get some rest."

Everyone leaves me alone, and I let rest take me. When I wake up again, my mind goes to Vivian. Something in me wants to recall the missing time, but I can't. What did I do to make her hate me so much? Have I forgotten it so I could forget what I've done? Damn it, I'm afraid to ask.

# CHAPTER SIX

## SIMON

Five weeks. I've gone through just over one month of therapy, both physical and mental. The hardest part is the day of the accident. Things all seem to be muddled when it comes to that day. Flashes of memories come to mind, but they don't make any sense. I have no idea what happened.

At this point, it matters because it seems that the person who ran me over is getting away with it. Everyone tells me that the woman who called 911 is the bitch who caused problems between Vivian and me, as if we didn't have issues to begin with. She claimed to have been on a date with me at first, but the police challenged her, and she backtracked her statement quickly, stating that she was only trying to make Vivian jealous. The bitch pissed me off.

There's a knock on my door, and my brother ducks his head inside. "Can I come inside?" Eric asks.

"Sure," I answer with a nod as I adjust my shirt, pulling it down my chest. I'm about to get to work for the first time in so long.

"Jack's here too." They both come inside, closing the door behind their dumb asses. My younger brothers are great guys and I don't know what I'd do without them, but they love to work my nerves.

"So, what's up?" I can tell this isn't just a brotherly checkup. Something is on their mind.

"We came to see how you're doing. How is the PT?"

I scoff because they're around often enough to see me improving, and I'm betting it's not my physical therapy they're here to talk about. "I'm down to two days a week, and I'm going back to the shop today." I've got so many classes to make up. With graduation around the corner, the school has allowed me to handle everything at home with online monitoring, and my teachers will make visits to test me as well. It's not as if I wasn't the number one student while attending the program, anyway.

"That's good. So...um...we wanted to talk to you about Viv," Jack sputters out. My shoulders tense, and the tightness in my chest expands.

My dad knocks on the door rapidly before coming in and interrupting our conversation, stopping my brothers from telling me about my future wife.

"Come on, Simon, it's time to go," my pops calls out.

"I'm coming," I mutter as he enters my room.

"Boys, you don't have to hover around your brother. He's doing a lot better, and he needs to get some work done so he can submit it to his teachers." That's the only good thing that came out of this. I have two classes in my final semester: one automotive class that is focusing on motorcycles, which I saved until last, and a final math class. The math one I can take online, and the motorcycle one is mostly online with submitting some of my work from the shop. My father set up a tripod for me to record my workstation. I had a late start to the semester, but they were able to let me slide because my grades are impeccable.

I nod to my brothers and walk gingerly behind my father. My injuries were to my left side. I had a cracked skull and a slice on my face as well as a broken arm and fractures from below my knee to my ankle. The scary part has been the brain bleed and swelling. It led to the two-week coma and then the memory loss. Unfortunately, I still don't have a clue who ran me over, and what's worse is that they don't believe it was an accident, from signs of acceleration.

I head downstairs carefully. Most of my injuries have healed, but it's just in case I get dizzy. I promised them that I'm nearly a hundred percent, but they aren't having it. My body aches, but it's to be expected.

"Before you head out, it's time for breakfast, Simon," my mother says. She sets a plate on the table in front of me. "Did you take your medication?" she asks as she lightly brushes her hand through my hair.

"Yes, Mom. I did take it. Thank you for the breakfast. It smells and looks amazing."

"Anything for you, sweetheart." She smiles, but it's not reaching her eyes. Something is bothering her, and it probably has to do with morning sickness. My parents are adding to the family, which came as a big surprise, so Dad's extra protective, especially after what happened to me. My mother was a wreck.

My dad wraps his arms around her waist from behind, snuggling her close. "Are you taking it easy, Dash?" he whispers in her ear.

"I'm fine, love. I promise that I'm taking it very easy."

"Sit, and I'll serve you some food before we get to work."

"So, Pops, are the cameras set up?"

"Yes, your station is all ready for your instructor to check in, but it will be at your request so he can't just have access when he wants. Also, he'll be stopping by from time to time as well."

"That's great. I'm not worried about any of that. I can't wait to get back into a steady rhythm with my hands again."

"You'll be back to normal soon." I nod and dig into my food. A part of me believes it. The only thing that hinders that belief is the lack of memories from that weekend. Since I've been back, I haven't seen Vivian. She never came back to the hospital or stopped by to check on me. Whatever happened, I did something to upset her, and it must have finally been enough to push her away for good. The thought of losing her forever burns a hole through my chest, marking my soul.

"You will," my father insists. "Even if the memories of that weekend don't come back."

"What if I never know who ran me over?"

"We're working on it. Trust me when I say we have our people looking into it. You won't have to know, and they will pay." His teeth clench so tightly with those words said with such finality that I'm certain it will end in death or maybe maiming for that person.

We chow down while my dad quizzes me between bites. I must have been starving because I practically lick my plate clean. Standing up, I place it in the sink. "I'm ready, Pops."

He does the same with his plate and then comes back and leans down to kiss my mother. "Take it easy, beautiful."

He drives me to the shop, even though it's within walking distance, because I need to reserve my strength. "Now let's see the setup."

My normal workstation has three different cameras—one above and behind my station, and two that are moveable based on the location of the vehicle I'm working on. The excitement builds in me instantly.

"So what do we have on the block for today?"

"We have to work on three bikes, four oil changes, six tire rotations. Mrs. Colson's car isn't starting, so we have to bring it in and run a diagnostic and see what's going on. Do you want to pick your project?"

"How about I start with the diagnostic and get my feet wet again?"

"Sounds good." He nods. Throughout the day, everyone stops by my station to say hello and check on me. They all offer to help, but I send them on their way. It takes a while, but I figure out what's causing Mrs. Colson's vehicle to stop running. She was out of gas was step damn one. She has a hole in her tank by the fuel filter. She reported that she had gotten gas two days go, and it was empty. Although, according to my tools, her entire panel was lit up like a damn Christmas tree. There are several things wrong with her vehicle. Who knows when she's had an oil change, all her tires are threadbare, and her engine is missing coolant. In this temperature, it's no wonder her vehicle hasn't exploded already.

"Pops, where the hell is her son?" I ask.

"He disappeared with the last of the inheritance she received from her husband's will."

"That bastard."

"Tell me about it. We're doing this on the house."

I nod. Mrs. Colson used to be a schoolteacher before retiring a few years ago when her husband died. Now, she's left with nothing because of her asshole son.

# CHAPTER SEVEN

## VIVIAN

"Vivian, dear. It's a surprise to see you here," Mrs. West says, catching me in the middle of the cereal aisle. Damn it. I don't have anywhere to run, because of course it happens to be the exact moment that two workers are restocking the shelves and we're caught perfectly in between them. I intentionally left my house in the middle of the night, way too late for me to run into anyone I know, or at least I thought so.

"Oh, hello, Mrs. West. It has been a long time. I hope you're well," I say, doing my best to show no signs of the pure discomfort I'm feeling.

"It has been a long time. You disappeared after the accident, but I can understand why. I'm sorry that you feel like you can't trust Simon, although we're positive he had nothing to do with that young woman."

I choke, in shock by her bluntness—something I should have come to expect. "It's not that," I admit.

"Then why?"

"It's complicated. We had a big argument, and we said things, did things. Then...I told him I didn't want to see him again."

"We all say things we don't mean sometimes."

"Yes, but then he left angry and nearly died. I'm sorry. It's my fault that he was out there."

"Vivian, no. Don't do that to yourself. Don't."

"I'm sorry. I have to go. Excuse me." I leave my cart and rush out of the store. My heart just aches. I'm nearly out of the store when I slam into Simon's chest.

"Whoa, whoa, Trouble. Who are you running from?" He looks over my head and around me with a snarl.

"No one. Um..."

"Tell me whose fucking face I need to smash in," he growls, staring at me intently. God, it's the way he looked at me at the hotel in his room and when Richie was talking to me.

"No one."

"Why are you lying to me? You hate me, but I'm not sure how to fix what I did wrong."

"Simon?" his mother calls out from behind me. Her distraction allows me to move around and leave before he can stop me. I have to get away and control my emotions. He thinks I hate him.

"Good night," I call out before sliding into my vehicle and driving away. I just can't deal with the feelings he brings out in me. It's so confusing. For some reason, he's under the impression that I hate him, but if he remembered that night, he would probably remember that I'm the one who led him out into the cold where someone struck him down.

I pull into the driveway empty-handed. As soon as I enter the house, my father raises his brow. "Sweetheart, it's ten thirty, and you don't have any bags from the store. What happened?"

"Um… they didn't have what I wanted?"

"None of it?"

"Um…no. I'm going to bed." I hang up my keys on the hook and go straight to my bedroom. I don't want to talk about anything, especially when it comes to Simon, who I haven't even begun to understand. It's been a month since he came home, and he looks incredible, handsome as ever, even with the scarring on his face.

I prepare for bed and then lie down and try not to let my feelings of guilt and heartache eat me up as I drift off to sleep.

The morning light floods through my window, and I'm dreading the questions my parents have prepared for me. There is no doubt my father told my mother. They don't keep secrets, and they do everything they can to protect me.

After I dress and brush my hair, there's a knock at my door. Damn, they didn't even wait for me to come downstairs. "Come in."

"Sweetheart, I got an interesting phone call this morning."

"From whom?"

"Penny Steele."

"Mrs. Steele?"

"Yes, she was doing some late-night shopping last night, and she witnessed a confrontation between you and Simon. She didn't hear it all, but from what she heard, Simon's under the impression he upset you."

"You haven't spoken to Dad?"

"No, he had to work last night, remember?" Oh, yeah. I'd forgotten. He hasn't had a chance to rat me out. I give her a summary of what happened, and she frowns at me.

"So you ran away from that boy instead of telling him that you're not upset with him? He's going through a lot, and you're letting him suffer."

"It's not that simple."

"No? Please explain why it isn't. What happened in Vail that he's forgotten?" I explained how he told me his feelings and how we kissed provocatively and his promises, but then we fought, and I told him I never wanted to see him again. She gasps at all the right moments but squeezes my hands and smiles as if she isn't bothered by the idea that Simon and I had crossed some lines.

"See, I don't know how to be around him. I feel so guilty that he's hurt because of what I said, but we fought, and now he doesn't remember any of it." I do my best to fight the tears.

"Is there a part of you that's mad at him for forgetting?"

"No," I deny too quickly.

"Sweetie, I believe you are. It's hard to say why he doesn't remember it, or maybe he has pieces he doesn't want to remember. You are definitely not the reason. If he thinks you're mad at him, I assure you it's not because he doesn't love you that the memories aren't coming back."

"I don't even know how to be around him."

"Well, I called Vanessa this morning, and she has a wonderful idea."

"What do you two have planned?"

"It's time for you to shake off this fear and pain. Simon needs you, and you need him."

"You're right. What do you have in mind?"

"She needs rest as the baby comes, and they could use help in the office. Abby helps, but she has school too. So, she'd like you to come after school every day to learn the ins and outs of the shop."

"Are you sure that's a good thing? I'll be invading his space."

"Yes, it's a great idea, and I'm sure under all that nervousness, you're thinking the same thing."

I blush because a part of me loves going to the shop despite him sending me away all the time. The way sweat covers his bare, ripped biceps as he works sends shivers down my body. "Whoa, young lady. Calm down. I can see and recognize that look. You have a couple more months of school left."

"I know, I know."

"Good. Now, Vanessa would like you to come over to the shop today around noon to get a feel for the process." I checked the time on my cell phone and it's already eleven. Dang, that's not a lot of time, but I guess that leaves me less time to chicken out.

"Um...okay." When I enter the kitchen a few moments later, my father walks into the house. "Hi, Dad."

"Hey, Princess. How are you doing this morning?"

"I'm great," I lied. I'm a mess. Seeing Simon again is going to be a shock to my system that I'm not prepared for. It's not that I don't want to throw myself into his arms and continue where we left off in his hotel room, but I'm not sure that will ever be possible.

The doorbell rings, and in walks Mr. West. "Hey, Wrench," my father says. They shake hands. "What brings you here?"

"Oh, Vanessa didn't tell you?" Mr. West said, smirking at me.

"No, I just got home."

"I'm going to help, Mrs. West out at the shop by working in the office."

"She has a car. You didn't have to scoop her up, Wrench," my mom says.

"I was at the hardware store, so I was driving this way, anyway."

"Good. Thanks for giving her something to do," my mom says, hugging my shoulders.

"Yeah, I think it will be good for the both of them," he says while giving me a knowing look out of the corner of his eye.

"I'm sure it's going to be awesome," I mutter. "What should I wear?"

"Do us all a favor, and nothing that's going to get other men killed," my dad mutters, shaking his head.

"Daddy, I'm a grown woman." I roll my eyes at him.

"I'm not talking about me. I'm talking about Simon catching any guys staring at you in tiny shorts or in a low-cut top." I blush profusely.

"Your dad's right. We've both been married too long and understand how my son is going to react when a customer's eyes linger too long."

I roll my eyes again, and Mom says, "They aren't exaggerating."

"He hadn't acted that way until that weekend, and he doesn't even remember behaving that way."

"Sweetie, just because you didn't see it, doesn't mean it didn't happen." My father smirks. My mouth falls open, and my mind practically explodes.

"I'm going to change. I'll be ready in ten minutes, okay?"

"Okay."

# CHAPTER EIGHT

## SIMON

I STARE AT HER WITH A BRUTAL DISCOMFORT BUILDING IN MY chest. Until last night, we hadn't seen each other since the hospital. Vivian had fled, running back home. I suppose the sight of me had been too much for her. She was so damn angry, and normally I would brush it off, but I can't. It's too fucking much to bear. Her sadness is killing me.

I'm not sure why I have this pain, so I push it away because a headache starts to hammer through my skull. Digging in my pocket, I open my bottle and pop two pills and then go back to my work.

I focus on the way my hands easily turn the wrench and not on the way her eyes had slanted with painful sadness. I look over at my father, giving him a simple nod, which sends him over to me. In a whisper, I ask him, "Hey, Pops, what is she doing here?"

"Her dad wants me to help her learn about the books for her classes." I wonder what she is taking this last semester. Then I recall she isn't taking any math, so what's the real reason she's here? I already know the damn answer. My parents are trying their best to fix us—to fix me. The last broken piece of me. The part that even I know only Vivian can mend. Maybe I'll never remember what happened that weekend, but it doesn't matter as much as learning how to win Vivian. To remember why she was so furious with me, more than any other time before.

"Oh," I mutter. My lips clamp together as I duck my head down toward the bike, refusing to look at her.

He grasps my shoulder and gives it a squeeze. "You need to focus on school. Everything missing will come to you. Just give it some time. She's not going to linger down here. I'm taking her upstairs." Upstairs, where he takes Mom to screw? An unexplainable possessive feeling comes over me, and I grow angry.

"Into the office?" I question, dropping my wrench.

"What the hell is that supposed to mean, Son?" he sneers, giving me a scowl.

"Nothing. Just nothing." Jealousy—a foolish sense of jealousy tears at my gut. There's no reason for it because my dad is obsessed with my mother, but that doesn't mean I'm not still suffering from those emotions.

"Yeah, that's right. Go get to work," he says with a chuckle.

My alarm goes off, reminding me it's time to turn on the cameras and check in with my instructor for class. My presentation with my teacher goes well for the first fifteen minutes, until I catch his gaze shift behind me. I pause in my explanation and turn my head to see Vivian walking up to Petrol with some paperwork. He's nodding, and they're talking. A low rumble comes from my chest.

"Mr. West? Mr. West," I hear my professor call out.

Finally my attention is returned to the screen. "I see you are easily distracted."

"I wasn't the one initially distracted."

"She was lingering in the camera's view. I assumed she needed something," he snipes back as if I offended him, and perhaps he'd been correct. Vivian was probably looking around to find Petrol and caught the instructor's attention. I'm just overreacting.

"Have you found out who caused your accident?"

"No. We don't have any access to the cameras, so we can't determine if there was a busted-up vehicle, and I'm sure they're protecting their own up there."

"Probably someone with a lot to lose. Can you determine what type of vehicle?"

"I don't remember the incident, but from the injuries, it was definitely a freaking SUV."

"So it should have a smashed hood and front end, at the very least."

"Yeah. No doubt." I didn't tell anyone that I had a Ford logo imprinted on my shoulder for a few weeks.

"Well, I hope you find them soon."

"Thank you. Me too. So, with regard to my assignment?"

"It looks great. You're proving why you're first in your class, even after everything you've been through. Keep it up. I'll check in next week. That one will be in person, so it's going to be at four instead of the usual office hours session." I would claim it's due to Vivian, but it was already on our schedules.

"Thank you."

"Have a good day, Simon." He ends the session first, and then I turn off all my monitors and clean up my space because I have three oil changes that are calling my name before lunch.

I can't help but twist my head around to see if Vivian is still near Petrol, but she's nowhere in sight, so I'm assuming she's back in the office. I get my ass back to work and keep my mind focused because that's the only thing that gets me through the day. The idea of Vivian talking to the other mechanics with her sexy body and gorgeous face... I'm going to want to smash something or someone's face.

"Careful, Son. You're going to actually crack that wrench," my dad says with a chuckle.

"Sorry, just thinking..."

"Well, I don't pay you to think. How many oil changes do you have left?"

"One."

"Your lunch is going to get cold if your ass doesn't get moving." He pats my shoulder and laughs before walking away. There's no sympathy anymore. It's back to work for me, and I smile because it's just what I need. I decide to skip lunch and knock out the oil change and two rotations as well as fixing two belt replacements. It takes me a little longer to do one because the fucker is in a tricky spot, but I get it done before two, and then I go around hunting for a drink. I'm thirsty as fuck.

I walk into the breakroom and see Petrol talking to Vivian again. "Don't you have work to do?"

"I'm on a break," Vivian says. Petrol takes off without daring to challenge me. He knows damn well that I'm not asking him a damn thing. This is my family business, which means it's mine, and although Vivian doesn't know it yet, she's mine too.

"Scaring off the guys?"

"They should be working, not trying to get you alone." She blushes, looking so damn beautiful that I'm doing my best to keep myself back and not give in to the longing that I have for her.

"Please, you're overreacting, Simon. They are just helping me with questions I have."

"If you have questions, you come to me. Okay?"

"You're busy. You have a lot going on."

I close the distance between us, sliding my fingers under her chin, cradling her jaw when I say, "I don't care. You come to me."

"Yes, Simon."

"Good girl. Now, excuse me. I'm thirsty, and as luscious as your lips are, now isn't the time." I gently push away from her and go to the fridge, snagging a bottle of water, twisting off the cap and guzzling it down quickly. The sound of her shoes padding away is the only thing saving her because now that I've quenched one thirst, my body needs to slake the other.

Ignoring the lust and jealousy that dominates me, I work even harder than before, making sure that I knock out most of the solo projects. It's almost three when I meet up with Axel and Petrol, who are working on a classic Mustang that needs a full rebuild.

"We're glad you're here. We could use your help."

"I'm finally done with my list."

"Did you hand all your paperwork in?" my father asks as he comes up behind me, handing me a sandwich. "Don't think I didn't notice you didn't eat. Any other time, I'd let that shit go, but you're on meds, Son, and that can't happen. We've all had injuries and know that you can't do that shit. Eat, help these guys for an hour, and then get your paperwork to Vivian. She's got a lot to learn, and we don't need to make her job harder than it is."

"I understand, Pops." The fucks around me smirk until he scowls. I muscle down the rest of my sandwich while my father lays into these assholes.

"That goes for you shits too. Any trouble out of you guys, and you'll find your asses unemployed and my foot up your rears."

"You got it, Wrench." We all get back to work for over two hours before I remember that I owe Vivian paperwork and am going to get chewed out. The customers receive their copies, but there are things I need to submit to the office. Most of it is done on paper so we don't ruin the tablets with oily or greasy hands. Fuck—not only was I going to have to face the love of my life, but now the wrath of my parents.

I rush to my station and snag all the filed paperwork in my organizer on my desk that my mother set up for me and then take the stairs two at a time. Knocking on the door is a standard operating procedure if you don't want your eyeballs ripped out of your head, or in my case, ripping them out myself. My parents have enjoyed many passionate moments in there. Hell, I might have been conceived in the office. A fucked-up vision of bending Vivian over the desk and joining the family tradition is something I can actually get behind.

"Come in," she calls out, and my hand just lingers on the knob like I'm terrified to open up. Since I take too damn long, she whips the door open. "Simon," she gasps.

I rub the back of my neck. "Sorry. I know I'm behind with the paperwork."

"Well, come in here already." She steps out of the way.

"My parents aren't in here?"

"No, they stepped out for a bit." She gives me a knowing smirk, and I know damn well that they needed their afternoon delight. Shaking my head, I laugh and hand her the documents. "So are these all the ones you had today?"

"Yes, but there's no charge on Mrs. Colson."

"Yes, your father has a note for me on that one. I've already worked on preliminary reports, but I need these." She takes the papers from me and walks back to the desk, taking a seat and organizing them in some sort of system.

"You've got everything under control already, it seems," I remark, impressed at the way she moves around the desk with ease. I've tried to keep things neat so my mother doesn't ring my neck, but when I'm left in charge, nothing looks that organized.

"Hardly. I'm over my head, but your parents are extremely laid back and are giving so much grace."

"Nah, they know you've got this."

"Thanks," she says, biting down on her bottom lip.

"Well, I need to get back to work." I rush out of the door like a fool just as she opens her mouth to say something. I turn back, needing to see her again.

# CHAPTER NINE

## VIVIAN

I RELEASE THE BREATH I DIDN'T KNOW I WAS HOLDING because my heart hasn't caught a steady pace yet. I've been waiting for him to come see me all afternoon after Mr. West had said he was coming up soon to bring me paperwork. My entire body has been alive with anticipation, and yet the moment the knock came, I practically leaped out of my seat.

This morning when he was talking to his professor, I couldn't look away as he leaned over the vehicle, turning the tool, the muscles in his back flexing. My thighs began sweating so much that I could feel the wetness sliding down them. I practically bit out a moan, but then I remembered why I'd come down there and went straight to Petrol to get some answers on his last tune-up.

Simon's surly attitude hadn't made things any easier. My body had only been more excited by his presence, and I nearly jumped into his arms, as if I had any right to do so. It wasn't the right place or time for any of that nonsense. Simon was healing, and so was our friendship, if you could even call it that.

I've barely taken a seat when the door to the office slams wide open. "Simon," I gasp, pressing my hand to my chest.

"Sorry. Didn't mean to startle you."

"It's okay. Is something wrong?"

"No, I just forgot to ask how your first day was." He gives me an off-kilter smile that I've seen him toss to his mom or sister when he's trying to get his way. I'm trying to not melt in my seat.

The brain cells in my head team up and finally work together to respond with a simple, "It was nice." He stares at me like he's hoping for more, so I continue. "A little confusing, but I think I can get it."

"Well, you're pretty smart. I'm sure you'll grasp everything quickly." He runs his hands through his thick, mussed-up hair. "How often are you going to be here?" I'm not sure if he's anxious for me to go or if he wants me here, so I reassure him. "Your dad said pretty much every day after school, but don't worry. I won't harass you."

He closes the distance between us, dragging me out of my seat so that we're standing dangerously close. "Vivian, you're not harassing me. I want to see you."

I shake my head because I don't believe it. At least, not entirely. I turn my head to gaze out toward the loading bay. He doesn't care for it, and he grasps my chin with his strong, rough hand, turning my face to look into his. "I know I've been a jerk over the years, but it's complicated."

"Is it because I'm too young for you?" He might not remember our conversation, but I do.

"For now."

I nod, and then confess. "I know."

He lets out a heavy sigh. "I'm guessing we've already had this conversation."

I gently stepped away, moving toward the sofa, taking a seat. "Yeah."

"That I can't remember, right?"

"Yeah."

"That's why you're mad at me?" he asks. His eyes were so soft and gentle as he wonders, and I don't know how to explain that I'm not quite mad, and at the same time I am.

"It's complicated."

His phone goes off. "Damn it." He pulls it out of his extremely tight jean back pocket. "Excuse me. My teacher is calling me."

He raises a finger, telling me to hold on a moment. "Hello, Professor Smith. Yes, yes, I'll be down there in just one moment." He leaves the office, forgetting to close the door behind him.

I stand up to close the door, but then my attention is immediately drawn to his gait. He has a limp, and it looks worse than it did this morning, but he tries to ignore the pain. I wonder if his parents know how bad it is. I watch him walk to the front where a woman in a tight pencil skirt with a sleeveless pale pink blouse that clings to her chest enters and smiles at him politely. She looks elegant and mostly professional, except for the obvious overly full set of makeup she has on in this brutal heat and the fact that she's one of his teachers. A deep-seated sense of discomfort washes over me. Is it a general jealousy of a pretty woman, or gut instinct? Then, her eyes roam over him, and not because he's recovering. No—she has that hungry look that I had this morning. It's clear she admires his figure, like all women notice a hot man in just a sleeveless shirt.

"Simon," she says his name in a coquettish way. I almost expect her to twist a strand of her hair around her fingers. She hands him a file folder, pressing her hand on his arm a little too friendly for my liking.

I can't handle it. He doesn't like men near me, and he gets growly. After what happened in Vail, I am about to put my foot down. I don't care if he doesn't remember it. I do. Before I can open the door all the way and go down the steps, they are interrupted by his mother. The flirty teacher quickly makes her exit.

And then Mrs. West drags him over to his station a little further before saying something that sounds like *what the hell* or *who the hell*, but I can't make it out. Mr. West comes into the garage area, and then Simon looks up at the office, catching me staring. He slams his hand down on his workstation, and I can see his mouth move to make out the words, *son of a bitch*. Is something going on between him and his teacher? Or was she just another woman interested in him?

I close the door and get back to work. It's not my business, and I have to remember that I work here and regardless of what is going on, Simon and I aren't together. At this point, we may never be. He can do whatever he pleases.

I barely sit back in the chair and start typing when the door slams open. "Would you stop fucking doing that," I snap at Simon. He's breathing heavily, staring at me like a crazed, panicked man. "Are you okay?"

"Am I okay? You're the one who's upset at me again."

I put my hand up. "Are you taking your medication?"

"I'm not fucking crazy, Vivian. We didn't miss your expression."

"I don't care what you didn't miss. I also didn't miss that your limp is more intense since this morning."

"Did you come to babysit me? Is that why you're here?" he snaps.

"Don't fucking turn this shit around on me. I'm just concerned, asshole. I won't give a shit, then. Limp, be in pain, and then go fuck your stupid slutty professor, okay?" He's on me in a heartbeat. My body is up and out of the chair. His hands are in my hair.

"You are such a damn brat. I'm not fucking anyone. I've never fucked anyone. I only want to be inside you, and one day soon, I will be. Trust me. I am tempted, and I think everyone is trying to push me over the edge. I'd love to bend you over this desk and fuck you so damn hard you'd understand that no one else matters."

"Then what the hell was that shit down there? If you want me, what is she?"

"A professor who just crossed the line. She had no reason to come here today. My final math class is online. There is no reason for her to show up, so I'm not understanding it either, but as soon as I saw her dressed like that, I knew damn well what her game was. I politely told her that I'm engaged to be married and not interested in anything except math."

"Why—did she think she had a chance?"

"She wanted to use my time off against me. What a bitch. I hadn't thought she'd come here or anything. It's all recorded, and she's a fool because she's married with kids." He shakes his head. I wonder how he knows so much about the teacher since he's not in school.

"It's in the school bio in the online course," he says, answering my unspoken question.

"Are you going to report her?"

"No. I'm not interested in causing any drama. I just want to graduate."

"That's wise."

"You have nothing to worry about, Vivian."

I nod. "We're friends, Simon."

"We're more than that, and you know it."

"Why the change? Do you even know why you suddenly stopped pushing me away?"

"I almost died." I nod, biting down on the edge of my bottom lip. He doesn't know that he let his jealousy give in and he showed me more of himself before pushing me away.

"I know. I can't forget it."

"Hey, what am I missing? What did I do?"

"I need to finish this paperwork."

Mr. West taps his hand on the door frame as he ducks his head inside the office. "Hey, you two. We've given you both enough time to talk today. It's time for you to head home, Vivian," he says. He looks knowingly at Simon. "Same to you, Son. You need to eat and get some rest. Don't even dare argue, either. I'm going to drop Vivian off, and you're going home."

"What about the work?"

"It will be there for Monday. My wife and I will be here on Monday morning to handle it, and whatever we don't finish, you'll work on it when you come in."

"Okay." I smile at him and walk around his body to avoid going near Simon.

Two months have passed, and I make trips only three days a week to the garage, pretending to actually care about learning the ins and outs of working in accounting and management when all I really want to do is see Simon. It's not like I don't enjoy it, but it's not the most exciting thing to do after a long day of school.

Every day, I watch as Simon puts in so much effort to physically return to normal. His muscles struggle, and fatigue kicks in faster than he wants to admit. It starts later in the day, and then he drops his tools. That's when he lets out a string of curses. One of the men has to get him to stop. They all know that he's one of the future bosses, but in order to be in charge, he'll need to fully recover.

I make sure to stay away when it happens because I don't want him to be uncomfortable. He always looks toward the office, as if he's afraid I'll see him falter. What he doesn't know is that I'd do anything to help him.

"How is it going, Vivian?" Mrs. West asks me as she rubs her baby bump that's growing larger every single day.

"Great, great," I answer way too quickly to be telling the truth.

"Come on, Viv. Please don't lie to me. Your mother used to hide behind that façade, and all it did was make things worse."

I nod knowingly. My mother reminds me often. "Yeah, she told me."

She pats my cheek. "So don't repeat it."

"Well, I can't just go moping around."

"Have you even spoken to Simon?"

"No. I want to give him the space he needs."

"What he needs is some attention and support. Why don't you bring him this lunch I brought for both of you and something to drink? Have a talk about nothing and catch up. It's not like you can't talk."

I dip my head, feeling too embarrassed. "I…"

"Do you still believe that girl…she already confessed that she lied…" That isn't the issue. I hate that girl, but her bullshit lies were far from my mind. Not her trying to fuck him in his room, though. I wanted to rip her hair out for that.

"I know that. She's a shifty bitch who is just like most women who try to get their clutches into Simon."

"Then what's wrong? Are you no longer sure about your feelings?"

I nervously dig my toe into the flooring, as if it will help open up a hole to swallow me.

"Talk to me. I promise it will help, sweetie."

"That's not it…I'm the reason he left."

"But you're not the reason he was hit, so stop it. We can't change what happened to him. If I hadn't demanded he go on this vacation, he wouldn't have been in the position to get hit either, so there is that. As his mother, I assure you that has been on my mind more times than you can count, so please stop. Go have lunch with my son before the food gets cold." She pats my cheek and sends me from the room.

I've never been more afraid of her than I am at this moment. Mrs. West isn't the kind to be calm when angry, so when her words come out soft and so gentle, I know that I better do as I'm told or there will be hell to pay. Who knew that in a matter of minutes, our worlds will just change all over again.

# CHAPTER TEN

## SIMON

It's been two months since Vivian started working at the auto body shop with us. We've been tiptoeing around each other after our last conversation. It's more like she's been avoiding me. I'm not sure where we stand, but I'm doing my best to give her the space she needs. Still, I'm feeling more like myself, even though I don't remember the accident at all. I can't remember the weekend and all the drama that led to Vivian hating me.

If Vivian knew how I was fucking obsessed with her but hid it, we wouldn't have been through all this. Maybe I'm paying for holding back my feelings. I should have confessed it a long time ago, but then I would be suffering. Every fucking smile she gives to someone else tears at my heart because I want them tossed my way. It's unacceptable that she can leave here and hang out with her friends, as if she's not torturing me all day long.

"Son, I'm going back home for a little while. I'll be back to check on payroll," she says, kissing my cheek.

"What was that?"

"Lunch." Her smirk makes me wonder what she's playing at by bringing only Vivian lunch. I love my mother, but sometimes she's a mystery that only my father understands.

My mother leaves out the back exit after coming from upstairs, having dropped off something that smells fantastic. My stomach growls, and I'm a little annoyed that she brought Vivian food and not any for me. I love my mother's cooking, and I only packed a shitty sandwich for lunch. My stomach rumbles, but I focus on my work project.

I'm in the middle of filming an assignment for my professor, but Vivian makes me so damn distracted, I forget myself. The semester is almost over. One more month, and I'll be done. I have to remind myself of that every time I get so wound up.

Then my sexy Vivian comes sauntering my way. I set down my tools and turn off the camera.

"Hello, Vivian," I grunt out, fighting the growing arousal.

"Hi, Simon. Your mom brought us some lunch."

"*Us* lunch?" She conveniently left that out. "Did you want to go upstairs and eat it in the office with me, or…"

"I'll join you in a moment. Let me wash up really quick." Fuck, I'm not wasting an opportunity to speak with her.

I walk back to my station to ensure everything is turned off. I hurry into the office, and she has it set up at the table my parents usually share their lunch at. "Mom thought of everything." We get through our meal, making small talk.

"How is school?" I ask her.

"Good. I'm almost done."

"Are you planning on becoming a baker?"

"You remember that?"

"I've known you your entire life, Viv." I shake my head.

"I'm not sure. I only do it for fun. I used to help out at the bakery."

"What stopped that?" She looks around the room.

"Oh. Yeah…" I want to say that I'm sorry about that, but having her here is so damn worth it.

There's a bag for cleaning up the food and as we do, I see a small emergency bag that says *just in case*. "Your mom was prepared for everything, including this?" She lifts out two condoms. I gasp and snatch them.

"I can't believe she did that."

"Are you kidding? I'm surprised your mother hasn't put up a neon sign that I'm up here and single."

I let out a deep rumble. "You're not fucking single, Vivian."

"I think we've been through this."

"Fine. We have no need for these," I say, tossing them in the trash.

"Well, I'm glad we cleared that up."

"Trouble, we haven't cleared shit up. We don't need them because when I get inside of you, I won't be sliding a condom on. You're mine, and I'm yours."

"Fuck. Why do you have to say things like that?"

"Does that bother you?"

"Yes and no."

"Tell me why, and maybe I'll let you go without a kiss like you need."

"Because you make me horny. That's the truth, and like you said before, I'm too young and we have too many unresolved issues." She might have turned eighteen when I was recovering, but she's still in high school and I'm in college, miles apart.

"I only said the too young part. The other shit I'd love to get through." I can't believe I did anything too serious because it's not in my character. Despite forgetting that weekend, it didn't mean I would have abandoned my morals. I wouldn't have cheated on her, and I wouldn't have dared to lay a hand on her, so there wasn't anything I could have done that wasn't forgivable, or so at least I believed.

"I told you the truth. Now if you'll excuse me. I need to use the ladies' room."

"Okay, but we're going to talk about this later." She slides right past me, brushing my shoulder, although she did her best not to touch me at all. I smirked because it wasn't like she didn't want my touch. If I wasn't afraid of pushing too hard, things would have ended different here today.

She doesn't come back right away, but I hear the door so I go greet the bastard so he doesn't meet my woman first. As I get to the entrance, that's when a woman I don't recognize enters the workshop, and she's dressed inappropriately for the weather and the shop.

A grumble comes from me because I have a feeling shit is about to go down. The look in her eyes is full of deceit and calculation. She quickly adjusts it when I say, "Pardon me, ma'am. How can I help you?"

"Excuse me, handsome, but my car broke down just down the road and I need a tow."

"Why didn't you call for one?" I question. Something about her feels like a fucking set-up, and a sense of unease washes over me.

She tilts her head and then pulls out her cell before she waves her phone at me. "It's dead. I guess I'm just having all around bad luck," she mutters, smiling at me with too many teeth. I nod and then I whistle—two heads lift up from the vehicles they're working on.

When they step over to us, they wait for my direction. "Hey, Petrol, Tommy. This lady...I'm sorry, I didn't get your name."

"It's Mackenzie," she says with a purr, attempting to flirt with me as she refuses to even look at the other two. I do my best to hold back the vomit in my throat. I'd been happy to have lunch with Vivian; now I regretted it as I felt it coming back up.

"No offense, pretty lady, but you're barking up the wrong tree," Tommy says with a chuckle behind his gloved hand.

"Why? He's clearly not married." She looks right at my hand, smirking with a brow raised.

"Should have tried another name. Where did you get that one from?" Petrol asks.

"Because that's his mom's name," my mother huffs, crossing her arms. Seeing my mother only makes the situation wilder. This woman is playing a stupid game.

A barking laugh comes from behind me, and I already know it's my father. "Nice try, little girl, but flirting with a man and then using his mother's name isn't the best idea, and we know damn well that's not your name."

"Hey, Pops," my brother says, walking into the shop.

"You," she hisses.

"You know her?" I ask them.

"Yes, she's from Colorado. She's the one who lied to Viv about being with you that night. Then, she had to take it back, otherwise she would have seen who ran you over." I remember hearing something like that from the police when they were questioning me, but since I had no memory, they dropped it. This was the woman at the center of it all. A deep rumble starts to build in my chest as my temper elevates, but I'm interrupted by Trouble.

"Bitch," Vivian hisses behind my brother, who reaches out and holds her back. The thought of my brother's hands on my Vivian sets my teeth on edge. Every single day, I fight this insatiable attraction to Vivian that I can't describe.

I stare at my brother's hands, and he visibly recoils, loosening up his grip, but then Vivian practically pounces, forcing my brother to react. My thoughts go haywire when Vivian's in the vicinity.

"Calm down, Viv. He's not interested," he whispers. She's going to get his ass beat when I get better, and he can almost feel it with the way he cracks his neck.

Damn right, I'm not interested, and I want this woman out of my family shop before I have her thrown out. "Take her back to her broken-down vehicle and see her on her way, please," I say.

I turn to the woman and say, "And ma'am, stay out of Steeleville. We don't need your kind here."

"What does that mean?" she says with a gasp, as if she's offended, but I don't give a damn. I'm already annoyed with the situation with Vivian, and now this woman from Vail is here to cause problems.

"No lying whores," Vivian answers, pushing against my brother's back, making me so fucking blind with jealous rage. It's foolish, but I should be the only one to touch her.

"Trouble," I snarl, getting more and more pissed that she's

in my brother's arms. I need to get to her, but then she lets me have it.

"Oh, so this is a fucking repeat. She shows up, and suddenly it's back to the old fucking Simon." The vitriol coming from Vivian's beautiful lips takes me by surprise. This woman must be the reason she is mad at me.

"What are you talking about?" I ask, needing to know what happened. There is no damn way I betrayed my woman. No way in hell.

"She's just jealous of us." With everyone around, this girl is doubling down on her bullshit after she made up a fake name. The dumb bitch has no idea how close Vivian is from going insane, and how close I am from letting her loose. I won't hit a woman, but I'm not afraid to send a Steele Rider bride after one.

"She has nothing to be jealous of. I don't know you."

"You still don't remember me or that night. Me leaving your bedroom, the hotel shower." Guilt floods me as a dream of me pinning Vivian to the hotel room door in a towel surfaces in my mind. Could I have mistaken the dream for a memory? No. I Googled the resort, and that is their room, but I wouldn't cross the line with Vivian, and I sure as hell wouldn't touch a stranger.

"So, you do remember her?" Vivian mistakes my guilt and snaps. "I was right the first fucking time." Right the first time? She shoves my brother away and rushes upstairs to the office, slamming the door behind her.

"Get her the fuck out of here, now," I bark. They march that chick from Colorado out of there.

"Damn it, Son. You better fix that shit. You were moving in the right direction."

"I put protection in there for a reason," my mom says.

"Dash," my dad snarls.

"What? Come on—he's your boy. We'll be new parents again as well as grandparents months apart," she huffs.

"At least they'll grow up close," I state.

"Not if you don't fix this."

I throw open the door to find her packing her bag while she does her best to hide her tear-stained face from me. Damn it, I fucked up. After all this waiting and healing, I forgot to stop being an ass. She's not a little girl anymore.

"Are you crying, Viv?"

"No, I'm not," she lies to me, quietly sniffling.

"Bullshit."

She whips her head in my direction, glaring with a mix of anger and pain. "Look, what the hell do you care? Mr. West, I don't want to see you anymore. Leave me alone." A wave of memories hit me at once. A brutal one practically slaps me in the face, shocking me like a cold splash of water.

"Wait. Say that again."

"Why do you care?"

"Not that part, the other one," I growl, inches away from her pretty lips. "Say it again."

"Leave me alone," she whispers, the vehemence gone, but the memories return. One by one, the entire trip to Vail washes over me. The two days of one bad event after another flood my brain, and then that bitch from the front desk who has just come into my damn garage using my mother's name because she's that fucking obtuse.

"You're mine, Trouble, but there's some important shit that I need to take care of before anyone is aware that I have my memory of that weekend back." I bend down and do what I've been craving. "After all this time, no more waiting, and no more forgetting. Don't tell me to forget you again, because that shit isn't going to happen." I fist her hair, tipping her head back, and kissing her lips violently. She moans against my mouth, whimpering as she clings to me.

Her words slip past my lips. "Simon."

"Music to my ears, my gorgeous Vivian."

A knock on the door interrupts us. "Son, we're sorry about the interruption, but Miles wants to meet us at the Clubhouse. He's been digging into your hit and run."

"That's good, because a memory is coming to me and an image of the bastard who ran me over is coming to mind. He's connected to the hotel and that broad that was here. Petrol should be taking her to her vehicle."

"They can't be that far."

"I'll call him." I pull out my phone and dial his number. The second he answers, I speak in a hushed, commanding tone. "Only yes or no answers."

"Okay."

"Are you still with that woman?" I say calmly.

"Yes."

"Good. Make an excuse to bring her back to the Clubhouse."

"Oh...Yes, okay," he says with a chuckle.

"Good. I need to call Law."

"Actually, he's by the vehicle, writing a ticket."

"Great. Offer her a drink. I don't want her to know anything about shit." I end the call and then turn my attention back to Vivian. "Baby, I've got to handle this. Stay here until I get back." I can see my mistake before the words fully exit my mouth, but it's already too late.

Her face hardens she bluntly states, "No."

"No?" I asked, knowing that I'm about to have our first fight as a couple.

She stepped closer, got in my space, looking deep into my eyes when she says, "You're not leaving without me. The last time this bitch got in between us and we parted, something bad happened." Her words come out hard and brutal, but underneath, I understand there is nothing but pain. We almost lost each other. I could have died and I sure as fuck lost my mind for a while.

# CHAPTER ELEVEN

## VIVIAN

HE CLAMPS HIS LIPS INTO A FLATTENED LINE, UNABLE TO DENY me even though he wants to tell me no, but in truth he knows I'm right. He runs his hand through his tuff of dark brown hair and sighs, "Fine, but you have to do what I say when I say to do it. Don't get pissy and be defiant because shit might get crazy."

Smiling, I kiss his cheek. "Okay."

Simon's father gives him a look full of pride. Simon pulls me in for a rough kiss and whispers, "Good girl." I blush and smile as he takes my hand.

Nuzzling on my neck, he whispers, "Do you want to get on the back of my bike, baby?"

"Yes," I answered as my body vibrates. The idea of being on his bike, my arms around him and our bodies so close makes me ache painfully.

"We'll see you all later," Simon says, waving them off. His dad goes to speak to his mom because he'll be joining us at the clubhouse, but she's obviously not going there.

"No detours," Simon's mother calls out with a giggle. "I'll close up the office."

"Thank you," I replied, feeling unusually bold at the moment.

When we arrive at the Clubhouse, I see several vehicles are lined up in the lot. So many Riders have gotten here before us, including Uncle Mick and Aunt Morgan. That bitch from the hotel is in deep shit now. I love it more than I should, but she's involved in everything that caused me pain.

"Please, let's have a drink," Aunt Morgan offers her. "What would you like?" Although she's being polite and it's nauseating to witness, I recognize it's just a ruse.

"Um…just water, please. Why are there so many people here?" She looks around nervously, knowing she's in trouble. The terrified expression on her face amuses me to no end and it's just the tip of the iceberg. I flex my fists, ready to punch her in the face, but I can feel my body being held back by my man. Damn him.

"This is the Clubhouse. There's always lots of people around here," Simon says, as if it's normal, but his words come out menacing. He has that tilted smirk that turns me on. It screams condescending asshole and yet I still could never get enough.

"Is this like a biker Clubhouse?" Does she really have to ask such inane questions? I roll my eyes and catch a smirk from Boomer.

"Yes, it is. Now, here's your water." She takes it from Aunt Morgan but doesn't drink it.

"Thank you," she whispers.

"You care to tell us why you drove all the way here just to have your car break down near Simon?"

"I think I should be going," she insists, trying to dig her way out, but it's like a mudslide and she's not getting out without our help.

Aunt Crystal crowds her in and blocks her exit. "You're not going anywhere until we get some answers from you." Damn, she is too bad ass. I'm sure Mrs. West wants to be here, but can't because she's pregnant. Wrench won't let her and I can't blame him one bit.

"I don't know what to tell you." Her body tenses because we all know she's lying.

"You're going to tell us the fucking truth, or you don't walk out of here at all," Aunt Crystal says, staring her down.

Sarah swallows hard, shaking nervously, turning to look at Simon for help. "I just wanted to see if he was okay. My father demanded that I stay away from him after I caused trouble at the hotel."

"You mean after you had him run down."

She looks at Simon again as she speaks. "I didn't run him over. I would never." I'm about to pounce on her the way she says it. The damn flirty tone is annoying as hell.

"You're the only one with fucking motive and opportunity."

"You're mistaken, Simon; I swear it. I only came up behind them and saw him on the ground." She might be right. It's not like getting hit by a truck makes Simon a reliable witness.

"Then you know who hit him," I snapped, teeth clenched as I thought about destroying her pretty face.

She pauses for way too fucking long. My father is standing between me and the woman on purpose because he's aware of my temper. Simon pulls me to his side. "Stay close to me, baby." He kisses my temple, which draws Sarah's attention, and the jealousy is in her eyes.

She nods. "I do."

A round of snarling growls and hisses with nasty curses comes from those in the room. "You bitch," I snap, leaping out of Simon's arms, but I'm too slow because he has my back and my father is blocking the girl from my wrath.

She raises her hands defensively. "It wasn't me, I don't even know the kid that did it, but he had one of our vehicles and he was with our lead ski instructor. My father had it recorded via one of our outdoor cameras and didn't want the lawsuit."

"That bastard said the security cameras didn't work,"

Wrench roared. The tension in him was palpable. Everyone in the room could feel the rage pouring off him.

"Cyber, can you hack it?" Boomer asked.

"Their system is a closed circuit, but we have our ways," he said, and I wondered what he schemes were underway. They weren't just going to let them get away with answers like that.

"So why are you here—spying for your family?" Wrench asked.

She dropped her head and then slowly raised her gaze, giving him remorseful eyes. "I've been feeling so terrible about what happened. It's all my fault. If I hadn't been flirting with him, none of this would have happened. I was just trying to get away from my father, and it all fell apart."

"And you thought that coming here, what? You'd be absolved of your crimes?" I challenge, wanting to punch her in her pretty face.

"No. I just wanted to see if he was okay and hoped he still hadn't gotten his memory back because my father is a very dangerous man."

Simon scoffs, and so do several others. He may be dangerous, but that's nothing. We've handled dangerous, because all the Riders are devious. They will make a fucking shining example of all these bastards, and they will start with the guys who came after Simon and then her father.

"Well, boys, it looks like you're all having a meeting and leaving me out of it." Miles walks in with his three-piece suit and a smirk. That man is something else. If there was any one of us who came from the original Riders with too much bravado, it's Miles. Then again, the man proves that he is exactly who he says he is.

"How the fuck did you know about this?" my dad asks, chuckling and shaking his head.

"Let's just say I was in town on other business, and the sudden scurry of Riders caught my attention."

"Mr. Ivanov?" the Vail tramp gasps. We all stare, wondering how she knows him. I'm sure Elsa wouldn't like that.

"Well, hello, Ms. Steiner," Miles says with pure arrogance.

"You know them," she states with pure accusation.

"Yes." The slight uplift of the corner of his mouth is the only giveaway that he's amused. Miles carries himself so stiffly that you can't read him unless you know him well. "By the way, I just came back from my trip to Colorado. Papa, this is for you." He tosses his father a flash drive. "It's everything you need." Cyber walks away with the drive and goes to the security office.

Sarah's mouth falls open, and her hand goes to her chest. "So you weren't planning on investing in my father's business after all."

"I invested, Ms. Steiner. However, business is discussed between men, not little girls. The only woman I discuss my life with is my future bride. Excuse me." He swiftly turns on his heel without another word in his three-piece suit and leaves us there with our mouths open while we're staring at Sarah.

"Oh goodness, that man is hot, but he's a grade-A jerk. He was even more rude than you. What am I, hideous?" she blurts out, shaking her head in amazement. She has no idea how serious Steele Rider men are about their women, and Miles Ivanov is no different. Elsa Martin has always been his even if she doesn't want to be. No other woman will do and this chick had no chance.

"Desperate is more like it," Petrol says. He's a Rider now, like all the other men here, too. I have to cover my mouth to stop from laughing, but several others don't let their manners get in the way and let out a couple of cackling howls.

"You would be, too, if you had a sociopath for a father." I can see the tension in some of the older men in the family, but fuck if I care. All I can think about is my Simon. If it wasn't for her, he wouldn't have been mowed down like he was a bump in the damn road.

"Listen, I don't give a fuck about your father. We need to get this shit done and my life with Vivian started," Simon says, giving me an intense stare. A deep rumble comes from my father beside us. I don't want to even glance at him because I'm sure he's not pleased and might even try to stop us. My eighteenth birthday is tomorrow, and it's not like girls my age aren't already banging their boyfriends. Simon's only three and a half years older.

"So who was the ski instructor that you mentioned?" Uncle Boomer questions, returning to the subject at hand.

"He's our star attraction, Thaddeus. All the girls love him, and the guys envy his game."

"And you don't know who the other guy was?" Wrench asked.

"No, but she knows him," she says, pointing right at me. The accusation is clear in her eyes.

"What makes you think I know him?" I ask, annoyed that she dared to make up some bullshit.

"You were with that guy several times throughout the weekend."

Everyone looks at me, and I have to think about who was there that weekend. "You couldn't be talking about any of Simon's brothers." I bite down on my bottom lip and then gasp, "Wait, are you talking about Richie?"

"Hell, no. Richie Henderson?" my dad asks.

"That prick. I remember now. Jack and Eric messaged me that they were stopping him from kissing you." I blush and duck my head, shame filling me.

Simon cups my chin with his strong hand and lifts my face to look into his eyes. I never wanted Richie; I just wanted revenge on Simon. "Don't do that, babe. I'm going to destroy that fuck, but right now we need to do something with her."

"What?"

"Don't worry, we're not going to harm you if you're telling the truth."

"We'll take care of her. You two head out and let us handle this," my father says.

My brow lifts, but my father just kisses my cheek and says, "You might be eighteen, but you still have to graduate high school, so I expect you home in a few hours, young lady."

"Yes, Daddy."

"Have fun, kiddos."

"We're going to have more kids around here soon," I hear someone tease as Simon and I walk out the door.

I blush. "Relax, Viv. As much as I want to fuck you so damn hard and deep tonight, I'm not. I'm taking you on a date, and then I'm taking you home."

"Are you serious?"

"Yes, I've stayed away and good all this time. I'll be a good boy for a little longer." I can't believe this. My entire body is vibrating for this man, and he's passing it up like he isn't given the pass to have me just where he wants me. I try not to let my doubts sink in, but they're at the back of my mind. Maybe I'm the one truly in love and he's just not that interested.

# CHAPTER TWELVE

## SIMON

I WANT TO FUCK HER SO BAD, BUT THERE IS NO WAY I'M letting my guard down when I have at least one enemy in town who could harm my beautiful woman. What the fuck could Richie have against me other than my relationship with Vivian?

We have a nice drive out through the countryside where I ask her an important question. "What do you want out of life?"

"A lot of things, but I'm not sure exactly what you mean? You have to be more specific. Are you trying to stop this before it starts?"

"No, no, baby. Not at all. I just want to make sure you know that this is it. There's no telling me you're not in it forever. We're young, and you're even younger. If you change your mind and want something more…"

"Simon. I've had time to think about that. More time than I care to think about it. While you were ghosting me and then when you were hurt, I was confused, deciding what path to take. I've got nothing. All my soul ever wanted was you. I don't even mind pushing papers around the office and updating spreadsheets, ordering more supplies as long as it means I get to be near you."

"What about babies?"

"Goodness. I want a bunch of them. My mom and dad couldn't have as many as every other Rider, but we were a happy family and I'm almost certain that my mom is chomping at the bit for some grandbabies."

"Hell, that's probably why your dad wasn't trying to drag you away from me."

"I think he's just tired of seeing me moping around."

"I'm sorry that I ever made you sad, Vivian. I'm sorry that I forgot a moment together. Truthfully, that delicious moment of you in my arms felt like a dream."

"A dream?"

"Yeah. I swear I thought I made it up. You have no idea how many times I..." I freeze, unable to tell her that I beat off to thoughts of fucking her like an animal with no concern for her safety or needs. My hunger and desire were all that mattered as I ravaged her.

"You what?"

"Viv."

"What? You what?"

My cheeks turn red, but I have to tell her the truth because I can't stand the look of concern and doubt in those gorgeous hazel eyes. "I stroked my cock to my sick thoughts of fucking you like a wild man. You think pinning you to the door intense? That was just the beginning. I've imagined you in so many different spots and so many different ways. You have no concept of how vulgar..." She launches herself into my arms, slamming her mouth onto mine. I pick her up and wrap her legs around my waist so our pelvises touch.

"Simon," she moans as she presses her pussy against my hard cock. Our clothes are the only thing that keeps us from going all the way.

"Viv, we need to stop or I'm going to fill you up."

"So do it. Why—don't you want me?" she whimpers.

"I don't want just a moment with you, Viv. I want you to stay with me. If I take you now, you won't be going home ever again." Besides, I can't tell her that I'm not strong enough yet. I haven't even spoken to the doctor about that since I've never had sex before. There's no baseline for my stamina, and my physical strength in lifting her, which I sure as fuck plan on doing, needs to be above par.

"Oh."

"Yeah, baby. So as much as I have to keep your panties on, it's only for a little longer. Tell your mom that there better be a wedding right after graduation."

"We can always run off to Vegas," she moans against my lips.

"Damn it, that's so tempting." I groan, grinding her on me until she shouts my name. My own orgasm soaks my boxer briefs. It's going to be an awkward drive home, but I wouldn't have it any other way.

As I hold her hand, I consider my options. We might have to wait for a wedding, but another idea pops into my head. Maybe an apartment would work.

---

"I NEED TO HAVE A WORD WITH YOU, RICHIE. YOU FUCKING tried to kill my son." The venom in my father's words are satisfying to see and hear as he steadily inches closer to him. Richie squirms in his seat like the little bitch that he is. He went for me when my back was turned and used a weapon much larger because he is a coward and too weak to face me head on.

"Why?" I ask, slowly shaking my head at this guy I hardly even know.

"Because I fucking hate you. It's bad enough that you have one of the hottest girls around chasing after you like a fucking puppy dog. But then the girl I'm in love with— you slept with her too."

"Vivian was mine long before your little fascination with her."

"I don't give a fuck about Vivian. I'm talking about Shelby," he scoffs.

"Shelby? Are you talking about the girl that hangs around with Vivian sometimes?" I questioned. I'm not even sure which one of her friends he's talking about. There are two girls, but I'm betting it's the one who always flirts and I sent packing.

"Yeah. You fucked my girl and knocked her up."

My father and I look at each other, and then we laugh so hard. When I finally catch my breath, I say, "You fucking idiot. I never touched that broad. Not on my life. Which is what you were willing to take from me, all for nothing."

Clenching his fists, my dad adds, "You should have gotten your facts straight before you did something stupid."

"I never touched that girl. In fact, when she flirted with me, I sent her with her tail between her legs because Vivian is the only one I want."

The color drains from his face, and the pain of his stupid decisions just wash over him. "What have I done?"

"Made a lot of stupid fucking decisions, is what you did."

My dad grips Richie by his hair from the fucking roots and yanks his head back. "Where is the other asshole?"

"He's still up in Vail acting like he didn't do shit," Richie grumbles. Clearly wishing he was there instead of staring at all his possible executioners.

"Why did that prick help you?" I asked, needing to know why so many people wanted to end my life. Sure, I had made enemies, but I hadn't even been in town for a day before I had people wanting to kill me.

"Well, he's my cousin, not even a good one, but he's all for some trouble. Besides, he'd do whatever the boss tells him. You pissed off the boss and he wanted you to pay."

"Well, everybody believes that you still don't have your memory back. They're banking on it."

"Well, now we have video evidence. And let's just say I'm feeling like the law is going to be my friend this time."

"Wait. You're not going to kill me?"

"No. We're going to have you arrested and charged with attempted murder."

"How? Your evidence is illegal, and you kidnapped me."

"Well, see, that's where you're wrong," my father adds. We didn't tell him that Miles bought out Steiner and his property, making the tapes and the system legally his. After a quick change of a couple of law enforcement officials, we are ready to lay into these assholes. No need to kill anyone yet.

Law comes in with his deputy and makes the arrest. As he leads him away, I catch his cold glare. "I need a word with you."

"Yes, sir." I'm just as large as Vivian's father, but that doesn't mean that I'm not intimidated by him. He holds my happiness in his hands.

"Why are you rushing to marry my daughter?"

"Do you expect us to live together and not be married?"

"You don't need to move in together."

I laughed in his face, even though I didn't mean to, but the man has a lot of gall. Any and all of the Steele Riders couldn't dare argue that my demand isn't even logical or necessary because at least I'm waiting. I didn't just fuck, take her home, and then marry her. No, there is going to be a wedding, and then I'll bend her into a fucking delicious pretzel.

"Are you suggesting that I…"

"Don't finish that sentence. I regret opening my mouth already. It's just that I'm not ready for her to be grown up."

"I'm sure no one is, but I'm in love with her and have been for a long time. I almost lost everything and nearly lost her. I can't wait for life to pass me by because there might be someone better for the both of us. I damn well know there isn't. She's my little brat. I've rented a condo, and I'm asking Vivian to move in with me. I know we both have class, but we're responsible."

He nods. "Take care of her."

"I will."

"Good."

We shake hands, and then I ask my dad and Law, "So, what are your plans with Steiner?"

"Him? We have a lot of plans with that asshole, but it's going to take some time. It seems his daughter wasn't lying. As much as you and Vivian don't like her, she's a real victim of his abuse. She was looking for a way out any way she could get it."

I huff because Vivian isn't going to like it. "Don't worry. Her mother will have a chat with her. Your mom and hers didn't get along before either. It took a big incident for the ice to crack in their relationship."

I'd forgotten about that story, but he was right. They hated each other, and Viv's mother hit on my father before just to make my mom angry.

"Well, I hope she sees it that way and things work out okay because I'm not willing to upset Vivian."

"Don't worry, I'll do it."

"I don't want her upset at all." He doesn't understand that I put my woman through enough, and seeing any pain in Vivian's eyes and heart is too much for me.

"It will all work out." I sure as fuck hope so.

# CHAPTER THIRTEEN

## VIVIAN

THE BLINDFOLD OVER MY EYES HEIGHTENS MY AROUSAL. "What are you planning to do to me?" I trust Simon, so I let him guide me safely wherever he wants.

"Welcoming you into our new home the proper way, Vivian." When he slid the black silk over my face, I had no clue that he would lead me to a condo. He doesn't remove it until we're in the bedroom. He strips off my dress and then my bra, leaving only my panties on. Then, with a light press to my chest, he sends me falling backwards onto the mattress.

The sheets are foreign to me, smoother than mine.

"Our new home?" I question as his hands roam slowly up my thighs.

"Yes. You said we should just move in together before we marry, and it's the best idea," he answers as he disperses little kisses up my legs. I've waited for this moment for so long; I'm both nervous and excited. My body doesn't know how to respond to the pleasure. It's all new and thrilling as he touches me and teases me, and I can't stop squirming.

"Simon, I need…"

"You need to relax, my beautiful woman. I've waited so long for this."

"So have I, and I can't wait any longer," I complain.

"You're going to have to or I'm going to hurt you, and I never want to cause you any more pain." He slips his fingers under the waistband of my panties and drags them down. He snatches my soul as he throws my thighs over his shoulders and loses all ability to go slow, his face pressing into my pussy and his tongue lashing at my sloppy cunt. My eyes roll back in my head as he licks me like I'm a two-scoop cone in the hot sun.

I clench my fists around the sheets and come hard. Then, he lifts, pushing the blindfold off my eyes. "Damn, baby. You are so damn sexy when you let go and trust me."

"I'll never doubt you again."

"Good, because this might hurt just a bit." I nod, knowing that he's not small at all and this would more than likely be less than comfortable. My mom warned me when she put me on birth control, but then she said that Simon loved me and would take care of me.

"I know. I'm ready, Simon." My hands run over his chest

and up over to his back. Damn. He is so built that my core is dripping.

"I love you, Vivian."

"I love you too." He pushed his way inside until his hips press against mine. I take a deep breath, relaxing. Immediately I feel the pressure, but there is no pain like I expected there to be. "You're so large," I blurt out foolishly.

"Thanks," he chuckles.

"Don't get a big head…oh never mind," I gasped, clapping my hand over my mouth.

"Your blush is so beautiful, Viv. You're perfect and I'm head is already big because I've got you and I couldn't be more arrogant about anything else in my life. You're my everything Vivian." I smile at him and clench my core around his length.

"Damn, babe. This isn't going to last too long, but I'm going to make our first time as special as I can."

He slowly pulls back, and then pushes his way back in. I gasp and sigh as he moves steadily faster. His lips brush over mine, kissing me so tenderly as he rocks into me. "Viv, you feel so good. Please let me know if I'm hurting you."

"No, it's perfect," I moan, clinging on to his body. The connection is too real and powerful and I'm finally understanding why I had to wait. I'd follow him around like a damn puppy dog just to cling to him. "I need you, Simon."

"Fuck," he groans, tipping his head and latching onto my stiff nipple and sucking it into his mouth. My back bows and I feel my body nearly come off the bed completely. The only thing holding me down is his weight. He brings his mouth up to mine, kissing me fiercely and we go at it some more. The sex getting more intense with every pump of his hips.

Our sweaty bodies grind together, chests brushing up against each other, causing so much tension. My pussy throbs, and I feel my orgasm pulsing at the surface and then I come violently.

Shortly, Simon follows me, filling me with his seed. We collapse together and wrap up under the covers. We steal kisses and cuddle for a long time until I fall asleep for a little nap.

---

I WOKE UP TO HIM KISSING ME. WHEN I DO, HE'S IN HIS JEANS and nothing else.

"Are you going to show me our place, or am I just trapped in bed all day?" I ask, staring at his gorgeous body. The scars from the accident haven't made much of a difference. If anything, they make him sexier.

"Well, I suppose you should get to know your home. How can you bake in here if you haven't even seen the kitchen?" he asks.

I narrow my eyes at him and glare, but it's hard to keep it up. "Oh, getting me in the kitchen is your plan. I see." I lean over and snag my dress from the floor, slipping it on over my head.

"Yes, barefoot and pregnant, too," he teases as he climbs onto the bed to nuzzle my neck. His scruff tickles as he kisses my throat, making me laugh for a moment, but my fears take over my joy.

"I hope we have babies." I can't hide the pain in my voice even though I try.

"Are you worried because of your mom?"

"Yeah." My mom had complications, but it wasn't like she was infertile. I'm sure it was a one-off, but it doesn't mean I don't worry.

"We'll make sure you're healthy through each and every one, okay?"

"Okay." He kisses me once more before slipping his arms around my waist and lifting me up over his shoulder. "Oh my God. Put me down, you big goon. You're going to hurt yourself."

"Yeah, not going to happen. I'm strong, and my physical therapist said so."

"Really? You asked?"

"Damn right, I did. I wanted to make sure I could easily flip you around."

"You told him that you want to toss me around?" I'm sure I'm beet red from embarrassment. There is no way he actually said that to the therapist.

"Not exactly, but I think he got the hint," he says with a chuckle.

I slap his arm and duck my head, shaking it in complete mortification. "Oh my goodness. I'm never going to be able to show my face again in the gym."

"That's good, because I might have to get a little too crazy if you did. There are way too many men in there." I look up at him and he actually seems dead serious about that.

"You are nuts," I exclaimed.

"Damn right. When it comes to you, I'm insanely possessive." He slides me down his strong, muscular front so I can feel every rippling muscle and his protruding length against his zipper.

"I'm not sure why," I say, guilt and doubt living in the back of my mind.

He cradles my face with his big, calloused hands and looks deep into my eyes as he says, "Because I'm in love."

"I love you too, Simon."

"Good, because I can't imagine my life without you, Vivian. Even when I couldn't remember that weekend, I couldn't picture any reason that was serious enough for you to be that angry with me. I knew that I'd never betray you because you were always meant to be mine. My dearest love, will you marry me?"

"Yes. Yes, Simon. I can't wait to marry you." We kiss and then his phone rings, stopping our interlude in the kitchen.

He pulls back, and I finally get to examine my new space. My mouth drops open, and I gasp. It's perfect. It's as if he had designed it for me, even though I know he didn't since these buildings have been here for a long time. Still, it's wonderful and has a massive double baking oven. I open up all the cabinets, looking around and inspecting everything with greedy, imaginative eyes.

All the while, I don't even notice that he leaves the room.

# CHAPTER FOURTEEN

## SIMON

MY PHONE RINGS, SO I PULL AWAY FROM VIVIAN. IT'S MY father, so I assume he's letting me know about the move. There's a lot to do in a short time and I'm already dragging my feet because I don't want to leave Vivian's side for even a moment. "What's up, Pops?"

"Steiner's dead," he states calmly though I'm sure he's anything but.

"What?" I ask in an angry hush.

"He died in a helicopter crash in the Rockies." I see Vivian digging through the cabinets, so I let her do her thing while I take the call, walking away so she doesn't listen in.

"I can't fucking believe it. Do you think it was a real accident?" My mind immediately goes to my friend who has ways of dealing with matters especially now that he has millions invested.

"I don't know."

"I need to call Miles."

"Go ahead. Don't forget you need to get to Law's place."

"I know. We're getting ready in a few minutes. Thanks."

"Congrats." Despite the hiccup, I can't stop the smile that comes to my face. There's nothing that could take the joy away from me when it comes to my future with Vivian. All this other bullshit is inconsequential.

"Thanks." I end the call and immediately video call Miles because I want to see his face.

"What did you do, Ivanov?" No need for a greeting because I'm not calling for niceties.

"I don't appreciate your insinuation, West. I didn't do shit."

"Are you telling me that this was purely an accident?" I look at him, and he shrugs. There is no artifice in his face or body language, but the man is a master liar and professional. He's been trained by mobsters in Vegas and has years of experience with the rest of the Riders to have learned so many tricks of the trade. I wonder if he's telling me the truth.

"I'm telling you I had nothing to do with his death. If it was me, I would have made it way worse. The bastard took the easy way out, actually."

"You think a helicopter crash was an easy way out?" I chuckled.

He nods slowly. "I would have tortured the fucker, but it's for the best because he was facing a long prison sentence. The charges on him were going to be insane, and I had enough to rack up decades' worth of charges."

"Is there anything else we can pin on that instructor?" I asked, wanting one of these assholes to pay.

"We have a couple of charges, although not much other than the shit we already have. Your attempted murder will get him twenty years if we can. I can make things happen in time, so don't worry. It's the little punk that bothers me. If he makes any moves, I'll have him taken care of."

"Yeah, I can agree with that shit." Richie tried to make moves on my girl and if it wasn't for my brothers, he might have been slick enough to get a little taste of her sweet lips and then he wouldn't have made it out of that clubhouse. He's lucky, I was feeling a bit magnanimous.

"Good. Now, I have to get back to work. My companies don't run themselves. Besides, you need to put some clothes on before you take any more video calls. You're lucky I didn't have my woman in here."

I laugh. "My bad. Talk to you later."

"Hey," Vivian calls out. I turn around. "Do you usually take video calls without a shirt?" Shit. I am lucky Elsa wasn't there either because Vivian would have had my head too.

"Sorry, Trouble. I usually don't, but something happened and I called to bitch Miles out. He also called me out for having no shirt on."

"Good. What if he had a woman in there?"

"Sorry, but you know he doesn't." I smirk at her because there is no way that he would.

"Elsa could have been there," she huffed, crossing her arms and making up a scenario that didn't happen.

"He wishes, but you're right, and it won't happen again, babe." I pull her close and kiss her nose.

"It's glad you recognized that I'm right. Now, when are we moving in?"

"The movers are on their way to your house in three hours. Your mom has already started packing, but we have to get over there and get your things."

"And you're dragging your feet? Where are my panties," she shouts, shoving me away and taking off running back to the bedroom.

"Baby, come back," I holler, pulling them from my back pocket.

She peeks out from the bedroom door. "What? We have to hurry."

"Looking for these?" I wave her panties in front of my face.

"Oh." She comes to stand in front of me and tries to take them, but I raise them out of her reach. "Come on. Why are you playing?"

"Because I don't like you with panties on."

"Well, I don't think you'll like it when I bend over, stuffing my boxes with the movers there and they can see my entire kitty."

I growl and pin her to the wall. Quickly, my fingers find her hole and I tease her clit. Working her pussy, I grunt and free myself. My mouth crushes hers, and then I warn her. "No one sees you like that. They can hear you orgasm with my name on your lips, but your body is mine. Always."

"Always." I thrust into her and fuck her roughly against the wall, giving no quarter as I dominate her, fucking at a punishing pace, each thrust hard and powerful. I know I shouldn't because she's got to be too sore, but I can't stop myself.

"I belong to you," she whispers against my shoulder before biting it and coming. I flood her hole, coming with her. Maybe I'll be less crazy soon.

# EPILOGUE

## SIMON

## TWO YEARS LATER

"Simon, we need to talk," Vivian says, entering the garage as I work on my motorcycle.

I stand up and wipe my hands on a shop towel. "Okay, baby. What's up?" I ask nonchalantly even though my body instantly hardens at the sight of her. She took the morning off, so I missed her even if it was only a couple of hours..

My sweet wife was fucking glowing from the summer sun kissing her soft cheeks. "There's something I need to tell you." She anxiously bites down on her bottom lip, gripping the hem of her skirt.

"Is something wrong?"

"I don't believe so, but it's a bit soon. I'm pregnant." My lips spread into a wide grin as the news registers in my brain. "You're having my baby," I say, the words coming out low in disbelief.

"I know I've only been off the pills for a couple of months, but maybe you have really healthy swimmers," she reminds me, as if I'm upset about our little one on the way. If I've given her that impression, I need to quickly correct it.

Cupping her soft cheeks, I whisper my love. "I love you, Vivian West, and I told you that I had no plans on taking any precautions now that the trouble has passed. Life's too damn short for that." She looks at me and smiles. Her gorgeous eyes brighten with joy as she stares into mine. "Come here." I slide one hand around her waist, pulling her firmly to my body. My other hand slips into her hair, tugging as I bring my lips to hers, kissing her roughly.

A deep cough comes from behind us. "I guess it's time for us to take a lunch?" Petrol asked.

"That would be wise," I growl against Vivian's throat while looking up over her shoulder at him.

"Gone," he swiftly replies before turning and speeding out and sending the others from the main area. I lead my wife to the office and close the door, locking it behind me. Within moments I have her splayed out on the edge of the desk, legs parted, panties gone and her dress up to her waist.

My lips twist up into a smirk as I stare at her shaved kitten. "Soon you're going to need some help, or you're going to have to let it grow. Either way, I don't mind." I lick my lips and run my tongue down her wet slit.

"Heaven help me, please don't stop. Please don't," she gasps. Her hand spears into my hair, closing her fingers around the strands and tugging. "Oh my goodness, Simon. It feels so gooood," she moans, tossing her head back. "Can't. Get. Enough your tongue."

She can't stop moaning my name. I'm so glad the shop is loud down below for all those who decided to work on the other side because my wife can shout the rafters down. Thankfully my parents are away with the baby.

Vivian's thighs open and close as she clenches and rocks her ass, but then backs off and worries about hurting me. I smack that round ass of hers. "Squish my face, baby. Smother me."

"I'm going to come right now." Her voice picks up and she presses her hand to her mouth, biting on the side of her palm to stop everyone in the shop from hearing her. I yank it away because even if they stayed or actually left, I don't fucking care. Let everyone hear my wife come for me. That's my number one job in life—satisfying Vivian West.

I lift up and free myself from these now constricting jeans and stroke my painfully hard cock, pointing it at her sopping wet hole. "Thank you, Wife," I state as I slide my way into her. She's given me another gift. Every day with her crazy ass has been a treasured gift.

"You're most welcome," she moans, wrapping her arms around my shoulders and holding on as I piston my cock deep into and out of her slick entrance.

"You're so damn soaked for me."

"Always."

"Only for me." I can't hide my possessiveness as I hold on to her hips and slam into her. The firm grip only drives me more insane. She's mine, and the thought of anyone coming between us makes me nuts.

She raises her hand and caresses my jaw and I lean into it, kissing the inside of her palm. "You know it," she responds, and I let go, flooding her pussy, unable to hold on for much longer, but we're not even close to done.

Before lunch is over, Vivian and I share two more orgasms as we kiss and celebrate our new path. Parents. I can't believe it, even though I've imagined this moment for so long, long before she and I were ever together.

We've babysat my new little sister many times for my parents to give us practice and them some time alone. The lessons were hard and fun. She had a lot of colicky times through the first six months, but she's a lot better now that she's a toddler. It was truly a lot of hands-on experience, and I'm grateful for it.

"Now, we should share the news with our parents," I say as I help her fix her panties.

"They are going to lose their minds."

"Your parents will certainly lose it," I say, dragging her onto my lap as I sit on my desk chair. Since they couldn't have more kids, it was only a matter of time until they were hoping the grandbabies would start popping up. Vivian only got off birth control two months ago. We were waiting until things settled with the assholes involved with my accident. With Steiner dead months after I gained my memory, Thad finally in prison for his role, and Richie having taken a plea deal, it was time for us to move on.

Ms. Steiner and Vivian will never get along, and I don't blame Viv for it. She's moved to another town where no one knew her. Miles was generous enough to let her keep a large portion of her father's assets, even some of the ill-gotten ones if she remained on her best behavior. The genuine happiness in her demeanor told me she was sincere. Even Vivian believed her, hatred aside.

Shelby moved to another town after word got around about why Richie committed the attack on me. Her lies and manipulations were out of control. Plus, the real father of her baby was the teacher who took them on the trip—Mr. Hart. He'll be doing some lovely time in jail. He blames her for seducing him, but he's a grown, married man and should have known better.

"What are you thinking about?" she asks, rubbing my scruffy chin.

"About how much has changed since Vail," I sigh against her hand.

She nods. "Goodness. A lot, but it's all for the better. Good riddance to bad rubbish, as they say," Vivian says, waving her hand.

"Wow, becoming a mom already."

She elbows me in the gut. I grunt, and then she gasps from thinking her little jab actually hurt me, so I let out a little laugh. "I should get back to work, and you need to get some rest."

"I should. Someone has been working me to the bone," she sighs, grinding her ass on my lap. I lift her off me and set her down on the sofa.

"Lie here for now. I shouldn't be too much longer, and then I'll drive you home."

"Sounds good, Daddy." We won't worry about her vehicle because we'll both be back tomorrow.

"Damn, baby girl. Don't talk like that. I have to get back to work sometime today." I adjust myself through my jeans, and she lets out a soft, musical giggle before falling asleep. My life has never been better, and I can't wait for what the rest will bring.

# EPILOGUE

## VIVIAN

## TWELVE YEARS LATER

"Mom, you're spoiling them," I say, setting down the grocery bags on the counter. She came over to watch the little ones while I went out shopping alone. I swear there wasn't a new dollhouse in her arms when she walked through the door this morning, and yet there is one sitting in the middle of my kitchen floor in the play yard with the two little ones. I leave the back door open.

She waves her hand at me, hushing me.

I walk back out to grab the last set of bags. "Mom, the girls don't need more toys," I sigh, unloading the bags onto the floor near the pantry door.

She scoffs. "It's my job as a grandma. It's in the description. Didn't you read it when you hired me all those years ago?" she answers, rolling her eyes at me. I can't with her. Sometimes I don't even know why I bother trying because she's not going to give in. It's been twelve years and five babies.

She stands up and starts helping me with the bags. "There's more isn't there?" I asked.

"Only for the older ones." I laugh because I'm not even remotely bothered by the spoiling. It saves Simon and I from having to do it. We do the disciplining and that's perfect for us.

"Are you staying for dinner?" I asked as I finished putting away the onions.

"I can't because the babies and I are going to my house for the night," she says, smirking at me while picking up one of the toys.

"What?"

"Yes, you and your hubby are going to have a night alone while we take the little ones."

"Are you serious?"

"Sure. Why not? We love having the grandbabies over. Besides, Daniella isn't breastfed anymore, so it's perfect. You don't have to worry so much, Vivi."

I set my hands on the counter and stare at my mom who is a darling. "I don't want you to feel like I'm taking advantage of you."

She scoffs, "Please. I'm so happy that we have so many little grandbabies to spoil." She picks up Daniella, holding her close. "Nana, loves her babies." We were all concerned that I'd have problems like my mom and that I'd have trouble with my pregnancies, but so far it's been easy.

"They love you too."

"Knock, knock," I look over at my back door and see my father waving.

"Daddy, come in."

"You know you shouldn't leave your door open like that," he says, wagging his finger.

I shook my head at him, frowning because he knows the house is well secured. "My gate is secure, and you knew the code to get in. Besides, the house needs some air, but you're right. Look what rabble just comes in here." I jab my thumb toward my father and my mother giggles.

"So are we snatching the babies today?" my father asked, rubbing his hands together.

"Yes, we are," my mom says, squeezing the baby.

"Do you want me to drop off the boys when they get off of school?"

"No, Simon should be getting them on his way home and then dropping them off. Let's get their things together."

"So he's in on this?"

"Yes, I stopped by the shop this morning."

"That's why he acting strange when I called this morning." He was almost too happy on the call. My heart pounded in my chest as I looked forward to a night with

Simon. We get our moments alone, but with so many children, it gets a little more difficult.

"Yep." It took about twenty minutes before I kissed my baby girls' cheeks and whispered goodbye until tomorrow.

As dinner roasts in the oven, I showered and prepared for my husband's arrival. I came down in a summery dress, just as the timer buzzed. I turned it off and set the pan on the stove to cool as the lock on the front door clicks and my heart does flips.

As soon as Simon's eyes land on mine, all thoughts of dinner disappeared. The lecherous look in his gaze shoots straight through my stomach and my pulse quickens. "Wife, what are you wearing?"

"You like it?" I choke out the words.

"Like is an understatement. I think you're trying to end up with baby number six." With every word, he moves a step closer. His keys hitting the kitchen table, eyes never leaving me.

"Maybe we can practice at the very least," I squeak out. He pounces and carries me to the living room where he shows me how much he loves my dress. It's on the floor in mere seconds. My panties are pushed to the side, and my hands are planted on the cushions while my husband is on his knees eating my pussy from behind.

"Fuck, baby. You taste so damn good. Keeping my dinner nice and warm," he growls against my cunt. I can barely hold onto the sofa. I grip the back and the seat as he devours me into a screaming mess. "That's a good wife. I love the way you taste. Time to fill you up. I didn't get enough this morning." He stood up and I heard his zipper slide down like a sensual warning of what was to come.

I woke him up with my tongue wrapped around his cock, making him come just as his alarm went off. "We have all night long," I moaned as he finger pushed into my hole, stretching me out.

"Part your legs, wife. I need it fast." I extended my leg over the back of the sofa while my other foot stayed on the ground, stretching me out. "Perfect." He shoved his length inside of me.

"Simon, babe. Fuck me." He drives into me wildly, fucking me until neither of us can catch our breath. We come together and he lowers my leg. We lean over the arm of the sofa onto the cushions with his chest on my back.

"Thank you, baby. I needed that."

"So did I."

"After dinner, do you want to go for a ride?" I smiled into the fabric.

"Yes."

We finally ate and spent a romantic evening together. The ride had been one of the best parts of the night. The air had been just cool enough to kiss my heated skin, making the stolen kisses perfect. I love these impromptu dates.

When we were in bed for the night, he said, "Just so you're

aware, my parents already want to claim the kids for Saturday night now."

"Are you serious?" I laughed.

"This is becoming a weekly habit," I teased.

"I'm not complaining," he growls, bending over to bite my shoulder.

"Neither am I." With a smile, I swiftly flip Simon onto his back and tease my husband into another round of hot sex before we pass out for the night.

In the morning as we get ready to pick up the kids and then take them to his parents, I suggest a trip, "With all these mini-breaks we should go on vacation one of these days."

"No, skiing," he blurts out.

"Definitely not." I kiss him and then walk out of our bedroom with a shake of my head.

THE END

# ALSO BY C.M. STEELE

### A Best Friends Duet:

Picture Perfect * Instant Obsession

### Best Friends Series:

Always You * His Dirty Secret * Sleep Tight

### Bianchi Crime Family:

Married to the Mob * Captured by the Mob * Owned by the Mob

### Cavanaugh Security Series:

Protecting Macy * Securing Blake

### The Cline Brothers of Colorado:

Whatever it Takes * Taking Whatever He Wants * Finding Paradise

### The Conti Crime Family Series:

Alessio * Dario * Enrico * Matteo * Gio

### Dirty Boss Series:

My Pet * My Cookie * My Flower * My Valentine

(Now on Audio)

### The Falling Hard & Fast Series:

Falling for the Boss * Falling for the Enemy * Falling Hard

### The Fiore Family:

Christmas with the Beast * Christmas with the Boss * Christmas with the Sheriff

### Gimme Series:

Sugar * Luck * Rain * Cream * Heat * Love

### Holly Hills Christmas:

Holiday's Cookies * Celeste's Secret * Bethany's Crush

(Now on Audio)

### The James Family:

No Choice * No Way Out * No More Waiting

### Keepsakes:

Keeping Blossom * Keep in Mind

### The Lamian Wars:

Bound * Reveal * Release

All Hallows Eve

### The Middleton Hotels:

Built for Me * Built to Last * Built Strong

Built Over Time * Built Overnight

### Nothing but Trouble Series:

Taking the Bait * Taking the Mafia Princess

### The O'Connell Family:

Claiming Red * Burning for Claire

Claiming Abby * Reminding Red

### Obsessed Alpha Series:

Stone * Cole * Graham

Theo * Maddox * Alessandro

Tony * Cormack * Cameron * Jake * Sawyer

### Reynolds Ranch Series:

Lara * Tobias

### A Rocky Start Series:

Rocky Waters * Her Rock * Rocky Start

### A Rough Hands Novella:

My Miracle * Nailing my Wife

## Say Something Series:

Say Uncle * Say Please * Say Uncle: Doggy Style

*Second Generation:*

Say Yes

## Seasons of Love:

Wet Summer * Autumn Falls * Winter Frost

## Sister Switch:

Testing Her Professor * Assisting Her Boss

## A Steele Christmas:

Mason's Winter * Perfectly Wrapped * The Company You Keep

## A Steele Fairy Tale:

My Gold * My Forever * My Property * My Prince Charming

## A Steele Riders Family Novella Series:

Sammie * Roxie * Mike * Dylan

## Steele Riders MC Series:

Boomer * Mick * Jackson * Doc * Beast * Ghost

Wrench * Blade * Boss * Cowboy * Law *Cyber

## Steele Riders MC 2$^{nd}$ Generation Series:

Will * Julian * Simon * Miles

## Southern Hospitality:

Down South * Gone South

## Sweet Temptation Bay:

A Taste Of Honey * The Mayor's Surrender * Trapped with my Stalker

## Sweetheart's Treats:

Sweet Surprise * Doctor's Orders, Sweetheart * Sweet Surrender